Lycan

Jan McDonald

Raven Crest Books

Copyright © 2012 Jan McDonald

ISBN-13: 978-0-9933747-5-3
ISBN-10: 0-99-337475-1

Even a man who is pure in heart
And says his prayers by night
Can become a wolf when the wolfbane blooms
And the moon is full and bright.
Anonymous. (The Wolf Man)

PROLOGUE

It was getting dark and the typical drizzle threatened to intensify. Jude Mason lay shivering at the edge of a pine forest, naked and unaware that he was being watched. Blood had congealed on his face and chest. He put his hand to his face and felt the growth of coarse hair that had appeared on his cheekbones. There was an alien feeling in his mouth, almost as if his teeth didn't fit. He ran his tongue across his slavering jaws and winced as the sharp points and elongated canines drew blood. He tasted the coppery tang of raw flesh and spat onto the forest floor.

The girl stood behind a tree. She knew only too well what was happening to him. She'd seen it before. Her brother Abram had suffered the same way up until the day he had died. The day he had been killed when the family were no longer able to protect him or those around him. The man was in obvious pain as he thrashed around in the bracken and the howl into the night chilled her soul.

The man tilted his head back and sniffed the air; his nostrils twitched as he detected her scent and he leaped to his feet. She stepped out from behind the tree, arm outstretched, reaching out to him.

His instincts were confused, her scent had fired something in him that his rational mind sought to obliterate and he felt the saliva pooling in his mouth yet his eyes were locked into hers. She was beautiful, a silky curtain of ebony hair and eyes to match, olive skinned with high cheekbones that gave her a haunting look, ethereal and yet earthy. Her entire appearance reflected her Romany origins.

"It's all right," she said. "I understand. I know your pain. Please let me help you."

He stood motionless, suddenly aware of his nakedness. She moved forwards unafraid. "Here," she said, holding out her shawl to him. "It's the best I can do for now. Come with me, I'll find you some clothes. I'm Sabine Wood, my family are staying close by."

He looked at her, puzzled by her reaction to his appearance, wanting to respond but all too aware of the blood on him. He turned away from her and ran through the forest. She watched him; even the loping gait was familiar. It was Abram all over again. She crossed herself and said a silent prayer for the good looking man with the dreadlocks who was on the same thorny path that had taken her beloved younger brother from her.

She could hear him crashing through the forest and the alarm of the wildlife as it scurried away from the beast that raged through the undergrowth. In the distance she heard the howl as clouds scudded away revealing the silver orb that had precipitated the transition from man to beast. She took comfort from the fact that there was only one more night left for the moon to remain full, one more night for him to suffer before he would be able to rest. She would search for him, seek him out and try and help him. For crazy as it was, in that brief moment when he had stared into her eyes and her soul, she knew that her fate was inextricably linked to his. For good or ill.

She drew her woollen shawl about her shoulders in an effort to dispel the chill that had settled on her, owing nothing to the rain. She wondered if she would ever feel warm again. She knew her father would have nothing to do with it, the memories of Abram were still raw with him and he wouldn't be willing to reopen the old wounds that had aged him an eternity and robbed him of the smile that had always been a part of him, now long gone. Whatever she could do for the man, she would do alone.

The rain stopped as suddenly as it had begun. Across the wild landscape of the Brecon Beacons where they merged with the Black Mountains, she heard the howl of torment and crossed herself again, praying this time for her own salvation.

Jude Mason loped towards the farmhouse, tortured by pain and confusion. He was breathless when he reached the door but he ploughed straight into the nearest outbuilding, crashing through equipment and timber as he collected what he needed. Less than an hour later all windows and doors in the farmhouse were nailed and boarded shut from the inside. He was going nowhere, able to harm no-one except perhaps himself and he didn't have a problem with that. He loaded his shotgun and placed the barrel under his chin. Unable to reach the trigger he looked around for anything that would reach and apply the necessary pressure. Not yet, but he would do it if it happened again. If once again he became wolf.

He was exhausted, filthy and thirsty. Running the kitchen tap he put his head under it and drank, allowing the water to run over his face and hair. Withdrawing his head he shook it, pervading the atmosphere with the overpowering odour of wet dog.

Unable to resist his overwhelming weariness, he lay curled up on the floor in the corner of the kitchen. Facing the door, with his shotgun within reach he fell into a fitful sleep peppered with dreams of rage and slaughter. And in his waking moments he prayed that his dreams were not in fact memories.

CHAPTER ONE: OLD CLIENT, OLD CHAIR

Acceptance had never been Beckett's strong point. Even in the priesthood he had questioned. His questions had never been answered, not by the Church. They didn't do questions, just authority. His answers had come from inside, from the still small place at the core of his being that held the key to everything. Ex Catholic priest with Catholic issues, guilt came as standard. Being a vampire wasn't going to come easy.

It had begun ten years previously, when he had cradled his sister in his arms as she died; the victim of the most ruthless and savage of his new kind. He hadn't known what to do, helpless in the trauma of it all, but knowing that to call the police or an ambulance would be futile, neither could help Grace then.

He had tried to pray to his God but the words wouldn't come, the light wouldn't come, the peace wouldn't come. His God was on a break. It was then that Lane had entered his life, melting in from the night, in control, taking over, containing his sanity. She was his saviour that night, preventing his mind from plummeting into the oblivion of the abyss, holding him in the reality of it. It hadn't been the dying that he couldn't handle, it was the rising.

Together they had kept vigil over Grace in death, standard Catholic practice, he was somewhere near his comfort zone. But when she rose, the slow motion movie that had played out in front of him left nothing of his old life, his old faith; all had gone in the slice of the scalpel that had severed Grace's head from her body. Madness had set up camp in him in that moment and it had been Lane that had given him back his sanity. It was that night that drove him.

And now he was one of them.

Beckett tapped on Lane's door and walked in, aware that she was alone. She flicked her long chestnut hair back from her face. "Morning, Handsome. Here. I have something for you." She held out a small velvet box. "If you want a different colour, it's no problem. I kept them clear for now."

Beckett took the box with a puzzled expression. He opened it carefully. Lane smiled.

"It won't bite," she laughed.

Beckett was staring down at a pair of contact lenses. "My eyesight is fine. More than fine. But you know that."

"They dramatically reduce the ultra violet rays and glare from the daylight. It doesn't have to be sunny to harm our retinas. Daylight is enough. The centre that covers your pupil is darkened to filter the light, like sunglasses. You will be glad of them Beckett. Trust me."

"You know I do."

"I have something else for you."

"Don't tell me, ear plugs to drain out all the extra noises."

She smiled affectionately at him. "Idiot. No. Something I've been thinking about for some time." She handed him a document from her desk. "I had it drawn up while you were asleep. Which incidentally, will be getting less and less."

Beckett took the document and began reading it. After several seconds he looked up at her with a stunned expression. It was a legal document naming him as a full partner in her psychiatric practice.

"But … you can't do this."

"That's funny, because I already did. As I said, I have been thinking about it for a while. You are an excellent therapist Beckett and you'll be an asset to the practice, especially now. Now you understand more fully."

"I don't know what to say."

"Say yes and sign it. It will make me very happy."

"I don't have money to put into the practice."

"I know that. I don't need money, Handsome. I need a partner. I want *you* for my partner. So, how about it?"

He grinned at her and ran his hand through his unruly hair. "Well, yes. Thank you. I won't let you down."

"I know that too. Here," she handed him her pen. He hesitated momentarily then grinned at her and signed the paper.

"So, the room opposite will be your consulting room. Much better than the rented broom cupboard you use at the moment. I've taken the liberty of having some business cards printed for you. They should be here later." She got up from the chair and moved in her elegant way to the Chippendale sideboard and poured two glasses of single malt. "Let's drink to it, partner."

He took the glass from her hand. "Partnership," he said.

He swallowed the fiery spirit appreciating at once the hints of peat and heather from the surroundings of its origin. His taste buds were alive and dancing. Another feature of the dark gift.

Beckett frowned momentarily and wafted the partnership agreement at her. "This is dated today and signed by your solicitor today."

Lane laughed, "You forget we have our own network and support system, Beckett. Doctors, undertakers, lawyers. Ailwyn Jones has been my solicitor for years. He doesn't sleep either."

"Ah. I see."

"I'm leaving my old consulting rooms in the town too. I've decided to work from here permanently. I want to keep an eye on my new partner. Speaking of which … Lucy is just finishing off emptying her desk of her personal stuff. The guy she's running off with, Jerome, Jeremy, something like that, is with her. She's off to Tibet to some commune or other, doesn't want me to keep her job open for her. Karma she says. More like drugs if you ask me. Still, they can both witness your signature."

She moved to the door in a heartbeat and called to Lucy and Jerome or Jeremy or whatever.

"I want you two to witness Beckett's signature on this document", said Lane. "And yes, I know he's already signed it, but only just. The ink is still wet. Here." She pushed the paper towards Lucy. She bent to sign where Lane was indicating.

"To save you the trouble of trying to speed read while you sign, it's a formal partnership agreement. Beckett and I are partners now."

Lucy grinned at Beckett as he penned his signature. "It will be great, I see it in your aura, Beckett."

Beckett rolled his eyes. Loopy Lucy, as he always referred to her, was about to launch into a plea to read his tarot cards. He smiled at her, "Luce, just sign the form, honey." Lucy signed in the appropriate place and her drippy looking boyfriend did likewise. They left arms around each other, eyes clouded with dreams of enlightenment in the far reaches of Tibet.

Beckett smiled at Lane. "Tibet? Really? Gotta feel for those poor monks."

"Okay, Handsome. Knock it off. She's been a good secretary, once you get past her little eccentricities. I hope she'll be happy."

"Me too." What are you going to do for a secretary?"

"The problem is solved. I've hired Angel. She helps out at the Sanctuary now and again. She's glad of a more permanent post. She'll be here later and you can meet her then. Think Darius only female."

Before Beckett could reply he suddenly pulled his cell phone from his jeans pocket. It rang.

Lane smiled at his anticipation of the call. He would be fine.

"Beckett," he said into the phone. "Yes, oh, hi there. No. No, it's not a problem. I see. Yes, of course." He smiled at Lane as he spoke. "I have changed my consulting room. I'm now at The Cedars on the Brecon Road." He laughed. "Yes, something like that. Four is fine. I'll see you then."

He clicked the phone off and returned it to his pocket. "A client of mine. Well, ours now, I guess. He wanted to know if I'd won the lottery. Strange, I haven't seen him for some time, a couple of months at least. He said he needs to see me urgently."

Lane put her head on one side and raised a quizzical eyebrow.

"I guess it's shared confidentiality now. His name is Jude Mason, he's an ex Special Forces guy. Came back from Afghanistan with Post Traumatic Stress Disorder; he's done several tours of duty out there and I guess the last one did it for him. PTSD is a bitch. Well, he's started to rebuild his life, moved into a farmhouse over on the Brecon Beacons and runs a pre-selection training school for anyone wanting to get into the army or especially into the SAS. So his clients are civilians and full time soldiers who want to get selected for Special Forces, private of course, nothing whatsoever to do with the MOD."

Lane nodded, she'd seen the destruction that war could do to a man's mind and at last PTSD was being recognised as a real diagnosis, it had come a long way from the First World War when it was called shell shock and often disparaged or ridiculed, the unfortunate sufferer often labelled a coward.

Just before four Beckett sat back in the plush leather chair behind the highly polished antique desk. He fidgeted, unable to relax and be at ease in his new office surroundings. He was still off kilter at Lane's surprise partnership offer and he missed his filing cabinet with its broken lock and his beaten up and cracked leather chair. He shifted his weight around the chair again and shook his head.

Exactly at four o'clock, a tall, slim, black eyelinered

Goth girl, put her whitened face around the door. Had to be Angel.

"Hi, Beckett. Mr Mason is here."

Another trip out of his comfort zone. His broom cupboard, as Lane had referred to his office, had no outer room and therefore no secretary, not that Beckett could have afforded one.

"Thanks, Angel. Er ... better show him in, then."

Angel smiled at his discomfiture. A state of being that dissipated the second that Jude Mason walked through the door.

Six feet four, muscles on muscles, latte coffee coloured skin betraying his origin of Hawaii and the deepest indigo eyes that sparkled and penetrated at first glance, and a set of dreadlocks that would make any Rastafarian proud; Jude Mason would be at home on any movie set.

Beckett was on his feet and welcoming him into his new office. The giant of a man was obvious in his inspection. He grinned at Becket displaying his perfect white teeth.

"You've come up in the world, Doc. Can I still afford you?"

"No extra charge, and it's Beckett, not Doc," he replied. "It's been a while, how can I help you?"

"I'm feeling worse. I'm getting more and more flashbacks and bouts of aggression that I can't seem to control. I thought about ending it all yesterday. Had the means to do it, but in the end, I was just too fucking weary. You're my last hope, Beckett. Weird things are happening to me, like all of a sudden I'm someone else. And I know how that sounds. The thing is ... the thing is, the flashbacks are more like waking nightmares."

"How do you mean?"

"I mean, I don't remember the things I see happening. That isn't usual, is it?"

"No, it's not, although hallucinations are a common symptom," murmured Beckett. He said no more, waiting for Jude to pick up his narrative. He waited.

Eventually Jude let his head fall towards his chest. "And I'm getting memory blanks."

"Memory blanks?"

"I think that … maybe … maybe I've been going out and not remembering it."

"What makes you say that?" asked Beckett gently.

"I suddenly realise that I'm muddy, or wet, and I don't know how I got like it. I woke up naked on the kitchen floor today, and not in a good way."

Beckett continued his gentle interrogation of the fragile giant, feeling his way through the tangle of confusion and scarcely hidden distress, getting nowhere and sensing the barriers shutting into place. After an hour and a half he said, "Will you come and see me again? Tomorrow? No charge," he said lightly in an attempt to ease his client's hesitation.

Without warning, Mason jumped to his feet and was heading for the door. "I've made a mistake. I'm sorry, Beckett. I'll be fine."

Beckett tried to read him but as yet he couldn't access another's thoughts. He was glad of it and yet he wished he could get to see past the guy's barriers. Lane would read him in a heartbeat. He knew better than to argue with a client in that frame of mind, so he simply said, "If you change your mind you have my number. Any time."

Mason nodded his understanding and left abruptly.

Beckett sat back in his chair, shifted his weight several times then frowned and crossed the corridor to Lane's room. He sensed that she was alone and after a brief token knock he entered her office.

"I need my chair," he said.

Lane smiled and gave the pretence of not understanding him. "Sorry?"

"I need my chair. My old chair. And my filing cabinet."

Lane smiled at him and nodded. "There's something sacred about one's chair. Okay. But I don't understand the bond with that wreck of a filing cabinet."

"I know it's not rational but I need my stuff."

"Of course it's rational. You need your old life around you until you can let it go. No problem. You'll need to empty it anyway. Is there anything else you need? Apart from your records that is."

He shook his head. "Thanks, I appreciate it."

She narrowed her eyes and he could feel her penetrating his thoughts momentarily then releasing him as she thought better of it. "What is it?"

"My client, Jude Mason. He just left abruptly, said he'd made a mistake and he would be fine. I'm not so sure; he seems to have taken a step backwards."

"Can we talk clients later? I have news but in the meantime, I want another blood sample from you. There are still anti bodies in your blood and I want as many samples as I can. There is someone I want you to meet. Dr Helena Bancroft. She's a geneticist who briefly worked with Greg Randall. Well, he's out of the picture now thankfully and so she has been promoted. We need her Beckett, if we are going to get the anti virus."

"Can she be trusted? I mean, I take it she's not a … one of us?"

"No. She's not one of us. She believes Greg was working on a cure for AIDS. No need to disabuse her of that idea just yet, until we know whether or not she can be trusted. The virus looks very similar and she may accept that it's mutated. She will also be very attracted to the funding that the council are offering along with the private lab facilities. She is first and foremost a scientist, filled with the need to find answers."

Beckett nodded thoughtfully. "It's a big risk."

"Life is a big risk Beckett."

"You're not going to … mess with her mind, are you?"

Lane laughed out loud. "No, idiot. Well not unless I have to."

"Because I've seen you do your Obi Wan thing. I'm

not comfortable with that yet."

"You soon will be. Now. May I please have your arm?"

She had picked up a syringe and tourniquet from the cupboard on the far side of the room. Beckett had seen her every move although human eyes would not have been able to track the movement.

"Dr Bancroft is willing to take up the post we have offered. Of course she doesn't know the source of the funding but I am fairly sure we can trust her."

"Only fairly sure?"

"Sure enough. For now."

CHAPTER TWO: UNCERTAIN FUTURE

They went to The Sanctuary in Newport and in the half light world Beckett sat looking up at the ceiling. It was painted off white against any glare that might damage his newly adjusted retinas, everything was muted, subdued, a twilight world that was to be his own for the rest of his days. And it looked as though they would be many. His last hope for a return to normality, whatever that may be, had died alongside its creator, Greg Randall or Santorini as the vampires knew him. The human anti vampire virus, H.V.V, had been still in its infancy when Beckett had ended the life of the thing that had taken Grace and catapulted him into the dark world of the vampire, the only one that knew of the anti virus because he had created it.

The Sanctuary was quiet as the grave, although he knew that not all graves are quiet. He had heard Lane's silent approach from the other side of the building. His hearing so acute that he could hear the buzz of electricity in the wiring, the quiet sigh of the girl at the desk in the reception area, tired and bored with nothing to do. He felt Lane's hesitation on the other side of the door, heard the deep intake of breath before she entered his room.

For the first time that he could remember there was uncertainty in Lane's eyes. An ancient vampire born of noble lineage Lane had survived for six hundred years. In the now, she was a successful psychiatrist with a flourishing private practice in the foothills of the Brecon Beacons. The Sanctuary was her brain child; discretely placed in the centre of Newport, it was a place of refuge for newly turned vampires where they could find donated blood and learn to handle their new life in a safe

15

environment without causing harm to any human. It was a blasphemy to the Born, those of pure vampire blood whose agenda did not include the Created, vampires who had been turned during a feeding frenzy.

Lane stood in silence, reading him, then she said, "Stage One has kicked in I see."

"Stage one?"

"Anger. Although as in all things in your new vampire being, everything is enhanced. Anger becomes rage. Denial becomes rejection. Revenge becomes obsession and finally acceptance becomes desire, though not in your case I fear."

"Never. I will never accept being one of them. There has to be something." He balled his fists and was on his feet and by her side before a human could blink. "I am not one of them. I never will be."

"Anger and denial rolled into one. OK handsome. Have it your way. But unless we can recreate the anti HVV, and we are a long way from that, Welcome to my twisted world. And now you need to feed."

Beckett strode up and down the small room, pulling his hands through his prematurely grey hair. "No. I've already told you. That's not happening."

"If you don't feed you'll weaken and die, just as a human would. If you stand any chance of working through this and helping us to put an end to the slaughter of innocent humans for the sake of their food, then you have to be strong. I guess you don't remember the emergency 'snack' you had in Greece?"

He spun around and was face to face, almost nose to nose with her. She didn't flinch, keeping her gaze steady and compassionate. Even though it was centuries ago, she still remembered the first hunger.

"What?" he demanded. What the hell are you saying? That I drank blood?" He shook his head. "No. Never. I would never do that. I would die first."

"You nearly did. I had to Beckett. You would have

died."

He looked at her in disbelief. "But you said a vampire couldn't drink the blood of another."

Lane put her head on one side and smiled fondly at him. "Not me. The boy."

Beckett narrowed his eyes and tried to search her mind but she was an ancient and he couldn't get past the barriers she had created to protect herself against such intrusion. Realisation dawned on its own accord.

"Darius?" he demanded.

"He's grown to care for you Beckett. I think he sees you as a hero. Though God knows why," she teased.

"Darius?" he said again, his disbelief and imagination preventing him from grasping the full import of what she was saying to him.

"You might like to say a thank you to him."

"He's here?"

"Waiting in reception and last seen chatting up Angel. Now are you going to be a good boy or do I have to get intense with you?"

Beckett had seen Lane 'intense' and knew her capabilities. He doubted his own new vampire strength would be a match for her.

In the dimly lit reception area of the Sanctuary, Darius stood unaware that Beckett was studying him closely. The brother of the vampire who had wreaked havoc in his life, Darius was on a crusade.

Back in his native Romania, his brother Andrei Marinescu had died a mortal then risen a vampire and slaughtered his mother and father without mercy. Darius had fled but had spent every day since then hunting him down. Finally, in Greece, he had witnessed Andrei's end, though not at his hand. Beckett wondered what would drive the boy now. He frowned at the thought of Darius saving his life. It wasn't supposed to be that way. He was meant to be the strong one, not the victim.

Darius became aware of Beckett's intensity and looked

up from his flirtation with Angel, the tall, slim, black eyelinered Goth girl who was apparently their new secretary. He tossed his jet black hair and grinned widely at Beckett.

"Ho. You look better than when I last saw you. You doing okay?"

Beckett nodded and walked towards him. He still wasn't used to the way it felt to move in his new being. He could feel the floor under his feet but it felt light, insubstantial somehow. And movement could be accelerated so that to human eyes it seemed that no movement of muscle and sinew was involved in crossing a room. He hadn't got the hang of that yet. He hadn't got the hang of a lot of things yet.

He gave a half smile at Darius and laid his hand on the boys shoulder. He almost expected him to flinch, to see him in a new light. A monster like Andrei. But the warmth emanating from Darius reassured him.

"Yeah, I'm doing okay. I'm told I need to thank you."

Darius shook his head. "It wasn't as though you were sucking at my neck or anything. That I may have had a problem with. Forget it, Beckett. Glad I was there. Don't sweat it man, you're a cool dude. For a vampire."

A hint of a smile betrayed Angel as she fought to keep up her Gothic alter ego, her cultured accent completely blew it. "Hey," she said. "You'll be my first." The smile threatened to break through again. "To get my blood that is."

Beckett's familiar frown creased his forehead as he turned to Lane, eyebrow raised in half question, half protest.

Lane moved silently to Angel's side. "Angel has received all the necessary counselling, Beckett. She's more than ready to be a donor for you. Our donors don't usually know who the recipient of their life force is, but you're different. You are the only one I know that carries some anti bodies to the vampire virus. Angel's blood is the most compatible to yours, without you having a twin brother that is. And I want as few contaminants in you as possible." She raised a hand to ward off further questions. "So Angel is coming with me and you can kick your heels with Darius. Maybe he can talk some sense into you."

She put a hand gently on Angel's shoulder and guided her towards the donor suite and closed the door behind them. Beckett wished he couldn't hear the conversation on the other side of it, the sound of the blood pounding against the tourniquet, the slow drip drip of the precious fluid into the collecting bag. He squeezed his eyes shut tight in an effort to block it. Darius broke the spell.

"Is it really tough?"

Beckett nodded.

"I'll get over it. What are you doing here? I thought you'd be back home in Romania by now."

Darius shook his head, "Na, there's nothing there for me. Here on the other hand, here I think I could be useful."

Beckett grinned at him. "Still fancy yourself as a slayer? Maybe I'd better watch out."

"If there's one thing I learned the hard way, it's the difference between a vampire movie and reality."

Beckett ran his fingers through his hair. "Well, this is reality. And it sucks. No pun intended. So, what do you think is here for you?"

"Lane has agreed to let me stay on. See the bigger picture. I want to help, Beckett. That's all."

Beckett nodded at him and turned away, unwilling for Darius to see the distress clearly displayed on his face. Further conversation was interrupted as Lane opened the door to the donor suite. She quickly picked up on Beckett's mood.

"Is there a problem?"

Darius shook his head. "No. No problem, eh Beckett?"

Beckett turned to Lane and tried to smile but didn't succeed. "No problem."

"Good. Come with me."

She turned and walked away from him her luxuriant long chestnut hair swinging as she moved. He hesitated before following her, watching her with different eyes. Another time, another place, maybe he and she? But this was now and he couldn't afford to blur the lines. Besides, two vampires in love were as explosive as nitro in a barrel of dynamite. He sighed, feeling the weakness taking over his body, feeling the blood lust rising, feeling his heartbeat slowing to an imperceptible tick. He knew he needed to feed.

"Okay, Legs," he whispered, calling her by the affectionate name he had given her ten years previously, an acknowledgment of her long slender legs that simply added to her elegance. "You win this one."

CHAPTER THREE: SURRENDERING TO SLAUGHTER

Jude Mason was becoming restless; he had slept fitfully since returning to his farmhouse at the foot of the Black Mountains where he ran his business. Now he was wide awake, filled with dark energy and he was hungry. Ravenous.

He pulled open his refrigerator, peered inside, and then slammed the door on it. He did the same with every one of his cupboards.

An overwhelming thirst raged through him and he felt as if he was on fire. He tore at his shirt and ripped it from his body in an effort to quell the burning. Sweat was running down his back and there was something lodged in the centre of his chest that almost seemed like a scream waiting to be released. He fought it.

He felt it rising again and swallowed hard on it, forcing it back into the depths. Military training kicked in, discipline was everything. He could beat this urge to scream.

But it was still there, growing in intensity until he felt that it would choke him. It felt like he'd swallowed a melon, whole.

He had found himself in terrible situations whilst a member of the elite SAS and had never felt rising panic, always disciplined, always cool. This was something else. Beyond control.

And that was the crux of the matter; he felt way out of control. Not knowing what to do next, not knowing how to stop the rising tide of panic and dread that was fostering the bloodcurdling scream that he knew would soon break free.

He was in pain then too, his jaw felt as if he'd been hit by a sledgehammer and intense agony filled his mouth, originating in the roots of his teeth. Teeth that all of a sudden seemed too big and too many for his mouth.

God in Heaven, they were actually moving.

Something was happening to his eyesight as well, his distance vision becoming blurred and indistinct.

Searing pain in his hands joined the frenzy then and he watched in horror as his fingernails grew while he struggled to make sense of it. Neatly clipped nails became long black talons and hair was sprouting up his fingers, over the backs of his hands and up his arms.

It was a long time since he'd prayed and he fought to find the words in the dense fog that only moments earlier had been his sharp mind.

And he knew he'd lost the fight.

He threw back his head and opened his mouth, his mouth that was too full of razor sharp teeth, releasing the scream that wasn't a scream.

The howl seemed to emanate from his very soul and it echoed and reverberated around the room, coming back at him, feeding on itself until he couldn't breathe.

It was over then, the pain, the sweating, the panic.

And the howling.

And what had been Jude Mason had become something else. He had become wolf and he needed to hunt.

He left the door swinging on its hinges and he was gone. Loping across the fields towards the rough heathered landscape dotted with white blobs, woolly white blobs that would become his prey and his food, he felt a surge of animal strength and energy that he had never known before. And a hunger for flesh, raw flesh.

His nostrils were twitching and he was sniffing the air; the scent of his prey was everywhere. The sheep scattered as he approached them but he ran now with wolf speed and deadly accuracy.

He brought the nearest one to him down with a single leap and in seconds he had ripped out its throat and his black claws were tearing at its flesh. His face was buried deep into the blood soaked carcass. Feeding in a frenzy of savagery and ravenous hunger, surrendering to the slaughter.

Temporarily sated he lifted his head from the gory mess. Cool raindrops were falling onto his bloody face, washing and cleansing. He drew a deep breath and howled into the lowering sky.

Somewhere deep in the darkness of his consciousness a light came on.

He stopped breathing and sat back on his haunches, looking around him and then down at the savaged sheep. And the howl became a pitiful whimper.

He was on his feet and running, he didn't know to where and he didn't care. He just had to run. And run.

He realised that he was on the top of Pen-Y-Fan, the tallest peak in the Brecon Beacons. It was a popular climb for walkers and climbers alike, but he had ascended the peak through the rough terrain and not on the path that spiralled its way to the summit, following the tough route that he took with his trainees.

The route replicated the famous Fan Dance of the Special Forces, which determined the fitness and navigational skills of the candidates. It was a route that covered twenty four kilometres over the rough terrain of the Brecon Beacons carrying heavy Bergen backpacks and rifles. Jude's trainees would ascend Pen-Y-Fan and then descend on the opposite side, and then reverse the route. Trainees that made it proved physical and mental strength and if they passed Jude's pre-selection training they invariably made the real thing. His trainees were allowed four hours to complete the course; Jude, the wolf, had made the summit in less than ten minutes.

He had raged through undergrowth and forestry and his jeans were ripped and bloody. He was thirsty and sniffed the air, the wolf in search of water, the man knowing that at the foot of the high peak was Upper Neuadd Resevoir. Beast and man arrived at the knowledge simultaneously. Wolf via his sense of smell and man from a memory that was buried somewhere in his clouded mind.

He knelt at the edge of the reservoir, back on his haunches, leaning forwards, head down and began lapping, his dreadlocks dipping into the cool crystal water. He drank until the burning fire inside began to subside.

When he stopped lapping at the water, his reflection was set in front of him and the myopic eyes of the wolf were beginning to find human focus again. His reflection came back at him like a bullet and made him recoil.

He looked down onto his muscular chest, glistening with sweat, water and blood. He held his hands in front of him and stared down at hands that had become his once more with neatly clipped nails, hairless but caked in drying blood. His fingers found his cheeks and apart form the usual stubble the layers of course hair had vanished.

His jaw ached as if he'd been chewing on leather for a fortnight.

He was up and running again. Running towards his den.

Once inside the farmhouse, he slammed the door and rammed the bolt home, panting and shivering. He grabbed his cell phone from the table and in a blind haze he punched a message. He threw the phone back onto the table and his eyes immediately fell onto his gun in the corner and he allowed his head to fall onto his chest in defeat. It was the obvious solution.

His hands were shaking and although he didn't realise it, he was crying softly. He took a deep breath and sat in the oak rocking chair by the side of the range.

During his service in the SAS he had taken human life on more than one occasion, but there had always seemed to be a rationale behind it. Terrorist cells, hostage situations, and some events that would never see the outside of a Top Secret classification. Now *he* was the threat. If he moved a few dusty files around in his brain, he knew what he had become and what he was now capable of without restraint. It had to end. Before he took an innocent life.

No sense in putting it off. Close range would be messy but he couldn't help that. One pull on the trigger and it would be over.

The barrel of the shotgun was long and he employed a long carving fork to reach down and push on the trigger, even so, it was awkward. The traditional barrel to the temple was out of the question.

He turned the gun around and rested the stock against the flagstone floor, barrel facing him. He leaned forwards, resting his chin over the end of the barrel. Closing his eyes he sent a silent prayer to whoever might be listening, swallowed hard, and pushed the fork firmly back on the trigger.

Nothing happened. No explosion, no scattering of bone and brain. Nothing.

He opened his eyes and stared at the gun as if it would answer him. Then he began to laugh, a crazy, hysterical laugh that was made of broken glass.

He hadn't taken the safety catch off.

Well, if that was meant to be a sign, he wasn't having any of it. He knocked the safety catch off and repositioned himself. Closing his eyes again he dispensed with the prayer and pushed down hard on the trigger.

Nothing happened.

He threw the gun sideways, rage and frustration boiling inside him. The cartridge had misfired. The Law of Sod in overdrive.

"Shit!"

He began pacing the flagstones, sweating again and a tell tale prickle in his jaw.

It wasn't fate it was a cock up. He wrenched the bolt open on his door and made for one of his several outbuildings where his equipment was kept. At the back of the brick shed he pulled out a tin chest and flung the lid open. He had found it in his cellar when he renovated the place. It contained a set of manacles on a chain, and other medieval looking bits and pieces that had been left by the previous owner. *Sicko* he'd thought at the time. But now he was glad of them.

He grabbed some huge nails and a sledgehammer. If he couldn't kill himself he'd bloody well make sure he wasn't going to harm anyone. Back inside he hammered home several wooden bars and rammed home the heavy bolt.

Down in his cellar he hammered the chain into the back wall, threw aside the sledge and snapped the first manacle around his wrist. It was tight and awkward but he managed to get his other wrist inside the other manacle and banging it against the wall he heard it lock. There was no key.

CHAPTER FOUR: THE HUNGER

Lane had her back to Beckett as he closed the door. He scanned the room in less than a heartbeat, immediately drawn to the mahogany coffee table set between two leather armchairs on which stood two silver goblets filled almost to the top with fresh warm blood. He frowned. He hadn't known what to expect, but it had been something more clinical.

Lane read him and smiled. "The treatment room is for emergencies, Handsome. You really want to feed in there?"

Thoughts flew through his head in a millisecond. Understanding came immediately. This was to be how he would survive until a cure could be found. No clinical transfusions. No distance. His nostrils twitched as the scent of the newly donated blood connected with receptors and neurons. The blood lust broke the barrier between Beckett and his new DNA and he lunged towards the goblet of blood, the musculature behind his canine teeth throbbed and pushed his fangs into place ready to pierce flesh. Everything swam before his eyes in a red haze.

Lane was across the room even before his new vampire sight could track her. Her arm around him, she guided him to the chair. "Steady Beckett. You will soon learn how to control it. Here let me help you."

She picked up the goblet nearest to him and held it up for him to drink. Rage and fear and grief welled inside him melding with the intense hunger that had coalesced in the centre of his being. He flung out his arm and dashed the goblet from Lane's hand onto the floor.

"*No!* Not now, not ever. Understand?"

27

He pushed her backwards and was out of the door in a second, past Darius who was still in the reception area waiting for Angel. Out into the night.

Darius was quick off the mark to follow him but a human trying to catch up with a fleeing vampire had no chance of catching him. He returned in minutes, holding up his hands in a gesture of failure. Lane closed her eyes and shook her head.

"Don't worry. I know where he'll go."

"Come on then, I'll drive you," he said.

"You'll need to, I heard him take my car. Hope he drives it better than he drives that heap of his own."

Darius gave a short laugh. "You know I still expect you guys to fly out of the goddamn window."

Lane smiled fondly at the young man, "I know we can move pretty quickly but flying is for the movies. We can jump higher than a human and move in the blink of an eye, and yes we can defy gravity for very short periods but flying is strictly for the birds. Come on."

"His place?"

Lane shook her long mane of hair back from her eyes, "No. I'm afraid we're in for a climb."

Darius looked confused. "A climb? It's dark."

"Won't bother Beckett, or me. You'll need to stick close to me in case you lose your footing."

"Where in hell are we going?"

"Hell is right. Beckett's hell anyway. We're going to climb the Blorenge." She smiled again at the blank look on Darius's face. "It's a small mountain outside of town. Beckett scattered Grace's ashes up there. It's where he goes when things get on top of him. It's where he'll go tonight."

They drove from the Sanctuary to the outskirts of Abergavenny in silence and left the car at the last possible place and began walking up the footpath. Lane stopped suddenly and turned abruptly to Darius. "You can either stay here or I'll give you a lift?"

Darius knew her meaning immediately. Lane would pick him up like a straw doll and be at the top of the mountain with him in her arms in a matter of minutes. He shook his head. "No thanks, I'll keep my feet on the floor down here. I don't think you need me anyway. It's only Beckett."

Her face was sombre. "It's Beckett in a rage of burning blood lust, out of control with grief. It's Beckett lost. I really don't know how this is going to end, but I know one thing. He needs to feed and soon. Or we'll lose him forever."

Darius nodded at her. "You go; I'll be ready when you get back."

They understood each other. Beckett had chosen the hard way. As he always would.

This time there would not be the finesse of a syringe or the Sanctuary, this time he would have to feed directly from a vein. From Darius.

Lane put her hand on his shoulder. "I hope Beckett knows how much of a friend you are."

"It doesn't matter. I just need you to tell me one thing."

Lane knew his fears. "There is no danger while I'm here. He won't take more than he needs. I'll see to that. And there will be no change in you, except for a small depletion in blood volume. You're healthy enough to make it back up quickly with plenty of fluids."

"You'd better get moving then," he said.

In a heartbeat she was gone, faded into the darkness that his human eyes couldn't penetrate. In minutes she was already a quarter of the way up.

Lane looked up towards the top of the mountain, using her vampire senses she found him, and her heart ached for him as she felt his torment. Her vampire hearing picked up the sobs and the gut wrenching cry into the night.

Minutes later she was at his side. His hands were in his hair as if to tear it from its roots and the tears were flowing freely down his cheeks. The look in his eyes was that of a condemned man. He searched her face, trying to read her but failing again. "What do you want, Legs? I'm beyond your help this time."

Lane didn't give way to the urge to hold him, standing fast a few feet from him and keeping her voice deliberately cold.

"I want to see you do it. That's what you've come here for isn't it? To end it all. Well, go on then. Jump. I'll just stand here and watch as your new DNA overrides your injuries. It'll be more painful than anything you can imagine but that's what you're good at isn't it? Suffering. But then I guess that's the years of Catholic doctrine trying to get out. Go on, Beckett, do us all a favour, after the injuries use up the last of your energy to heal themselves, you'll fall into the long sleep and there will be no waking you from it. I'm here as your witness." She paused. "What are you waiting for? Apart from the shattered bones, ripped flesh and spouting arteries, it'll be a breeze. The easy way."

His sobbing had subsided and suddenly all his anger and fear filled him and there was nothing else. He lunged at her and his hands were around her throat and he was squeezing, his thumbs pressing hard against her windpipe. Lane didn't move, she simply stood locking her eyes into his own crimson veiled orbits.

As quickly as his rage had welled inside him, he felt the last of his energy flutter and fail. He dropped his hands and lowered his head. He turned away from her, his hands covering his face.

"I can't," he said in a whisper.

Her arm was around his shoulder then, "Of course you can't Handsome. You're Beckett."

"I'm so sorry, Lane. I don't know what came over me."

"It's the hunger, Beckett. You have a choice, feed or die. It's that simple. I know you better than you think. You aren't going to give in to this because we both know that you are the only hope our kind have of reversing what has happened to you and hundreds of others like you. And while it is a slim hope, it's all we have. Now, are you ready to do what you have to?"

Beckett sagged visibly. He was weak and he knew it. Lane read him again.

"Don't worry Handsome. I've got it."

She picked him up like a small child and took the mountain in minutes. Darius stood near his car peering into the darkness. He straightened as a familiar glimmer alerted him to Lane's approach, then she was at his side with Beckett in near collapse. He fell against Darius as Lane released her hold on him.

Darius caught him as he fell forwards. "*Déja vu.*"

"We don't have much time. It's not like before, this time is has to be straight and it has to be now. Can you do that?"

Darius nodded, "You know I can." He pulled open his shirt to the waist as Lane lifted Beckett to his feet again. Darius tilted his head to one side and closed his eyes. "Is this going to hurt?"

She leaned forwards and pierced the vein in Darius's throat with a small, glittering lancet. Droplets of blood appeared on his skin and slowly began to trickle down into a pool on his chest. Lane dipped her finger into the crimson pool and softly placed it against Beckett's lips. He opened his eyes and shook his head. "I can't," he said brokenly.

Darius grabbed his arm. "Sure you can Beckett. This is a one and only deal, so you'd better make the most of it. This is getting kinda tedious you know."

He grinned at Beckett and the blood ran faster. It pooled and glistened and Beckett had no choice. His hunger had to be assuaged.

CHAPTER FIVE: CHAINED

Jude had stood for as long as he could and then sagged against the wall; supported only by the manacles, his shoulders pulled nearly from their sockets, head fallen forwards. It was coal black inside the cellar not acknowledging day or night.

Outside the darkness had enveloped the welsh landscape, and the moon was riding high in the night sky, and even in the darkness of the cellar, Jude knew it was night.

He had suddenly become wide awake, a strength coursing through him like he'd never known. A low growl started somewhere deep in his throat, vibrating his upper torso. The growl became a snarl as he yanked at the chains.

And there it was; the tingle in his mouth, the pain at the roots of his teeth as they shifted and grew. His hands and upper body began to burn as they became covered with course dark hair and his nails were once again merciless black talons.

Just as his distance vision had been blurred and fuzzy during the day, now at night his eyes were able to penetrate the darkness.

He felt his fury rising to a crescendo and the manacles around his wrists had left blood slicked hair all over his wrists and hands where he had railed against the chains.

Flecks of white foam sat at the corner of his mouth and he gave way to the torment, thrashing around in a futile effort to free himself. He had done too good a job.

He stopped as suddenly as he had begun, his eyes scanning the dark, his nostrils twitching and his ears pricked and scanning around like radar. Someone was outside.

He lunged forwards, only succeeding in making the manacles bite deeper into his wrists. Then he recognised the scent of whoever was walking around outside, he'd smelled it before. His mind was a kaleidoscope of images and memories, swirling and vying for ascendancy to his conscious mind. He saw trees and moorland and he felt himself running, running through undergrowth and laying down in bracken, fighting his demons, thrashing around. The image of him smeared in blood and naked made him halt. Would she venture inside, and if she did, would she be foolish enough to come down into the cellar?

He tried to remember her name, the beautiful gypsy woman who had stepped from behind the tree, but his mind lay dormant in a murky fog. He thought she'd been kind to him, with an apparent understanding of what was happening to him.

He remained still, unmoving, unwilling to make any sound that would alert her to his presence in the cellar. He sensed her still outside, hesitant.

He felt his heart pick up pace and strength, its beat rapid in his chest, thumping against his ribcage. Then as suddenly as it had begun it ended with a pain akin to a hammer blow centrally in his chest.

He refused to cry out, biting into his lip to stop it. The pain eased, melting away like old snow. And then he passed out.

Sabine stood at the side of one of the outbuildings, listening and watching, waiting for a sign that she was in the right place. The door was shut and she could see that the windows were boarded from the inside. She had to be careful; she remembered what happened when Abram had been confronted by strangers when in the middle of his wolf phase. It hadn't been pretty and had resulted in the bullet to the head that had ended his misery.

In the distance, she heard the blast of a shotgun, a farmer putting a half dead sheep out of the misery that Jude had left it in. There was no movement from within the farmhouse. She waited for an hour and then made a decision. She would talk to her father after all even though he was likely to be angry at her. Anything that brought memory of his beloved Abram back was taboo. But he may know what to do better than she and she suddenly felt nervous. She would come back and continue her vigil later, for now her father's wisdom seemed the best way forwards.

The three caravans were parked close together in a small dip in the harsh terrain, a small stream running close by. They were modern caravans but her father still referred to theirs as the vardo, refusing to relinquish what remained of their heritage. Occasional words had never changed, remaining in their original Romanian or Romany.

Her father was sitting on the steps to the vardo, puffing on his old pipe his face devoid of expression. Since Abram's death they had left their community and more or less isolated themselves, banished by their own kind, travelling with Sabine's uncle and two cousins who had chosen to stay with them.

She walked up to her father quietly and he opened his eyes, sensing the presence of his daughter as she stood watching him cautiously. She didn't want to cause him pain but feared she would, needing his advice which she knew wouldn't be what she wanted to hear. But there was a chance that he would help.

"Hello Bato," she said softly, using the Romany word for Father. "You were miles away. Was it pleasant where you were?"

He gave a half smile, as much as he could manage these days. "Sabine, where have you been?"

Her hesitation made him put down his pipe on the step beside him. He pierced her with brilliant dark eyes as she stood allowing his appraisal.

"What is it, child?"

"Bato, I don't want to cause you pain, but I fear I will. I need your wisdom on a matter that will bring back dark memories. I have come across a man who is in desperate need of help. I fear he is as Abram was. Varcolac." Varcolac, the Romany word for werewolf hung in the air like a thundercloud.

He didn't speak, just lowered his eyes and stood up slowly. He went inside the caravan, his vardo, and closed the door behind him. She heard the lock click into place. She had her answer. She was alone.

CHAPTER SIX: NEW HOPE

Back at the Cedars, Lane said, "So, tell me about Jude Mason," flicking the ash from her cigarette into an ornate marble ashtray.

Beckett wrinkled his nose, "I wish you wouldn't."

"I know you do, but it's hardly going to kill me now is it? Nor you now."

"You always say that, but it's antisocial."

Lane laughed aloud at him. "That's good. I'm a vampire, policing the world of human killing, blood drinking vampires who often have to be killed and smoking is antisocial? Give me a break, Handsome. So? Jude Mason?"

"As I said, he's ex SAS, been to hell and back in Afghanistan. He came back after his fourth tour of duty with PTSD, medically discharged on a pension from the force and living up on the Brecon Beacons. As I said, he's tried to rebuild his life by setting up a pre-selection programme to tie in with the rigours of selection for the Special Forces. Completely private and doing okay. Not making a fortune but making a living. Typically of ex Special Forces, except for a few that have cashed in with books, he's reticent about what happened to him. Something massive to push him over the edge I think. I thought we were getting somewhere when he suddenly stopped coming to see me. You know the rest."

Lane was thoughtful. "Does he not want to talk about it or does he not remember everything?"

"Both I think. He's in turmoil. That much I sensed from him. And it didn't take the vampire in me to sense it. It's hard Lane, to separate the therapist instinct from the vampire."

"Then don't. Use them in conjunction with each other. You are what you are now, Beckett. So roll with it. I know you aren't reading people yet, but when it happens. and it will, it won't be a question of can you but it will be more about suppressing it until you really need it. You may be able to help this guy better if you allowed yourself access to his memories, though I realise that hasn't fully developed in you yet. My thoughts on that are that the anti-HVV is suppressing it for now. Maybe it's a blessing or maybe it's a curse. But one thing is for sure, one day you will look into someone's mind and see their most private and hidden thoughts and fears."

"That is not a day I look forward to, but I'll deal with it when it happens. I wonder if he would see you? In conjunction with myself if you like. I'm sorry to ask you but I'm afraid for him, Legs."

"How afraid?"

Beckett hesitated. "Fairly afraid. For now."

Lane smiled at him and the corners of her emerald eyes crinkled. Her parted lips displayed the sharp white canine teeth that never receded completely. Those that didn't know her could be forgiven for thinking it gave her a predatory look. Mostly it just made her look sexy as hell.

"Well, partner, if he agrees to come back, I'm happy to give it my best shot."

Beckett appeared relieved. "Thanks. I haven't forgotten what happened the last time I asked you to do this."

Lane pulled a wry face, "No. But here we are. And you know what, Beckett? It's going to be okay."

Beckett appeared to relax although she could feel the tensions and struggle within him. He was such a stubborn son of a bitch.

"You have a contact number for him, I take it?"

"Yep, I have his mobile number, although he doesn't answer it. I keep getting his voice mail. At least I did before today. I'll try him again."

"Later then, Handsome. Give him time to think about

things again. Right now, we are going out."

"Oh?" his interest piqued.

"Time for you to meet Helena Bancroft. At her new lab."

"Where?"

"An annexe to the Sanctuary." She put up a hand to deflect his protests. "There is no access to the Sanctuary from it. She doesn't know yet what she's dealing with, but she has a mind like a bacon slicer and I don't think it will take her long. Long enough I hope to gain her trust. And I think that will have a lot to do with you, Handsome. You need to work your charm on her."

"Now wait a damn minute! I'm not playing Romeo just to deceive her. Bloody hell, Legs, where did you hide your ethics this morning? And anyway that Darius's department."

"Don't flatter yourself Handsome. I merely meant for you to be your natural charming self, not seduce the hell out of her. I'm banking on you appealing to her humanitarian instincts as a doctor. There's something about her, I don't know. I think you'll like her."

Beckett tried not to look grumpy but just managed the little boy lost look that made Lane laugh inside.

"Come on, we'll call in to your old office on the way back and collect all your records and anything that you want that will fit into my car, which won't be a whole lot. Darius has arranged for your old chair and that damn filing cabinet to be collected and brought here. Now, be a good boy and stop sulking. If you're really good, the doctor may give you a lollipop."

Beckett burst out laughing. The first time that he had really felt mirth since he couldn't remember when. "You're really good for me, Legs. What the hell would I do without you?"

Lane put on a mock serious face and shook her head. "I really don't know. It's beyond me."

Their easy mood and relaxed friendship continued

during the short journey from Abergavenny to Newport. However, Beckett's mood fell as they approached the area of Danse Macabre, the nightclub that had been owned by Darius's brother the vampire Andrei Marinescu and the scene of carnage that had left him turning into what he had become. A vampire.

Lane remained silent, feeling his emotions, reading his thoughts, and flippancy had no place there, only quiet understanding. Beckett had withdrawn again and she left him in his own darkness. His fragile barriers were up and although she could penetrate them with ease, she granted him his privacy.

It was Beckett that broke the silence.

"That place needs burning to the ground."

"I know how you feel, Handsome but we need to keep our eye on things and if the Born go underground it will make the job harder. God knows it's hard enough."

"I doubt God has anything to do with it."

"We're back to that are we? I thought you'd made your peace with the Big Guy."

Beckett gave her a puzzled look. "*The Big Guy*? Hell, Lane. You know how I feel."

"Sure I do. But I also know what happened when you prayed for Kat back in Greece. I know it gave her peace in her soul. You can't tell me you didn't feel it."

"As I recall, you weren't there."

"That doesn't mean I didn't feel it. I felt the shift in the energy, felt the presence Beckett and you'd better start to accept it. "

"Spoken like a true Catholic."

"Up yours. Just for now, can we leave this? There are more important things to concentrate on right now. So if you can't get over yourself for a minute, I'll drop you off right here."

She shocked him with her intensity and as he studied her closely he could feel the tension, feel her uncertainty and there was something else. He could feel her deep longing for a cure although she was way past its help; she yearned to be able to help those that it would. There was a flash in his head, like an arcing of electricity and he 'saw' her, tending a newly turned vampire and weeping. The image disappeared as quickly as it had arrived. The moment he had dreaded had come, her barriers were down and he had read her momentarily.

His voice was thick with emotion as the remnants of her grief still remained. "I had no idea. I'm sorry. You're right I'm being selfish. Come on then, Legs. Let's go see the scientist geek."

Despite herself, Lane laughed aloud. "I'm sure she would love that description." She pulled the car up at the kerbside and switched off the ignition. "So. Are you ready for this?"

"Hell, yes."

They didn't speak as they past by the entrance to the Sanctuary, unseen by those who didn't need to know, disguised as it was behind an innocent Indian restaurant. Beckett closed his eyes as he pondered on his last visit.

At the outer door to the new lab, Lane took a card from her pocket and swiped it through the digital lock. "There's one for you too," she said. Beckett didn't reply.

Inside the entrance hallway a steep flight of stairs rose at their feet leading to the lab which occupied the entire upper floor of the building. Movement from above told them that Helena Bancroft was hard at work. Lane took the stairs two at a time and her movements were only visible to Beckett. He still had remnants of belligerence so he climbed the stairs slowly and deliberately, consciously locking out the woman above. He needed to make a statement as he had no idea where this encounter was going to lead him.

Inside the lab a white coated woman with cropped, spiky red hair was bending over a microscope. Beckett noted the high heeled black leather thigh boots and short skirt. The open lab coat revealed a voluptuous figure.

Large amber earrings adorned her lobes and his nostril twitched as he detected her expensive perfume. Lane smiled as she read him. "Not the geek you were expecting, Handsome?"

Beckett frowned. She laughed.

Helena Bancroft looked up from the microscope. Her expression changed instantly and her fury was obvious in her emerald eyes that were only a shade away from Lane's. She stood up abruptly and her high stool fell backwards and clattered to the floor as she directed her fury at Lane.

"*What in God's name **is** this*? Don't take me for a fool Dr. Dearing! How dare you assume that I would simply accept your story of a mutated AIDS virus? I believe I deserve more respect than that. Explain yourself! And I warn you, if I don't like the explanation I'm walking out of here and going straight to the authorities with this. For Christ's sake, the virus cells are being killed off and then regenerating! Have you any idea what the implications of this are? *I demand an explanation. **Now**.*" She slammed her fist onto the workbench causing a rattling of glass tubes.

Lane retained her customary cool exterior but Beckett sensed her rapid thought processes and her instant assessment of the raging redhead with elfin features in front of her. He waited for her Obi Wan trick but it didn't come.

Instead she walked casually towards Helena. Not for the first time Beckett found himself watching her lithe catlike movements and the swing of her chestnut mane. As always he found himself admiring her.

Lane's hand was outstretched and she was smiling her reassurance. It seemed to have the effect of calming the woman. "Helena, this is Beckett. He is infected by this virus and needs your help. And there are many others out there like him. Now if you are prepared to open your mind, I will tell you exactly what this virus is."

Helena Bancroft's expression remained hostile but she bent forwards, picked up her stool and sat squarely on it, facing Lane with folded arms. "You have precisely two minutes. Then I'm walking. Starting now."

Beckett smiled inwardly at the woman with attitude, *Way to go Doctor*. He waited for Lane to come up with a reasonable explanation. He was shocked at her words.

"Greg Randall started this work because he had a vested interest in it. AIDS research was a cover for his real work. This virus and a potential cure. He's dead as you are aware, what you don't know is the fact that Greg Randall had a secret. He was a vampire. As am I, and as is Beckett, though he's only recently been turned. Randall had developed an anti virus which was showing great promise but his work died with him and all that is left are the anti bodies present in Beckett's blood. It's why we need you to continue his work, because without a successful anti virus this world will become the feeding ground for ruthless and vicious vampires. Does that explanation satisfy you, Doctor?"

Whatever Beckett had expected as a result of Lane's handling of Helena Bancroft, it wasn't what followed. She visibly relaxed and sat in silence for a moment reflecting on Lane's words before rising from her stool and approaching with hand outstretched towards him.

Beckett took her hand and nodded at her, "Dr. Bancroft."

"Helena," she replied. "If this is true and really it's too far fetched to be anything other, we'll be seeing a lot of each other." She turned to Lane. "What you tell me has to be the truth because it is so unbelievable. You should have told me in the first place. It might have saved me a whole lot of being pissed at you. A waste of energy and a waste of my valuable time. Perhaps we can start again. From the beginning. I need the full picture." She paused, "I take it you won't bite?"

Beckett smiled at her. "Well, that went well."

CHAPTER SEVEN: RELAPSE

They remained with Helena for two hours, telling and retelling the events that had led to Beckett becoming a vampire. Lane's history in particular seemed to fascinate her. Second only to her love of science and medicine Helena Bancroft was fascinated by history and Lane had lived through six centuries of it. Born Leonora Di Toledo and marrying into the Medici family she had been witness to world changing events. There had been a surprising acceptance of the hidden world of vampirism and no reference to the myths and legends that fed Hollywood and literature. For Helena it was a medical challenge that she was avid to try and get to grips with.

Beckett was wary of her complacence but Lane was constantly reading her and she seemed to trust the young doctor. It had to be enough for him for the time being.

The journey back to Lane's home had been quiet although not uneasy. Beckett had fallen into a distant mood and Lane left him in peace. Unwilling to read him but sensing his dark thoughts, she knew there was little that could be said. He had to come to his own peace with who and what he was.

When they arrived at the Cedars Beckett looked pale and tired. He would need to feed again soon and Lane didn't relish the struggle she would have with him again.

"You look tired," she said. "Why not go home. Angel is still busy notifying your clients of your new office and you don't have any appointments this morning. If anything crops up I'm sure I can handle it. If I need you, I know where to find you. I do know where to find you, don't I Beckett?"

"You know you do. Don't worry, Legs." He turned to

leave and in a split second, a searing pain elicited a howl of agony and brought him to his knees. Lane was with him in less than a heartbeat. She picked him like a rag doll and laid him on her brown leather Chesterfield. There was no need to call for Angel or Darius, they had heard Beckett's scream from the other side of the house and burst through Lane's door only a moment later.

"What the hell …?" demanded Darius.

Lane ignored him directing her attention to Angel. "I know you gave only yesterday but he needs more. He needs more and he needs it now. Will you?"

Angel nodded her understanding. "Of course."

Lane had been anxious about Beckett's deteriorating mood and his obvious need to feed more frequently than usual. She had put this down to the antibodies still present in his blood. The only time she had seen agony on the scale he was now displaying had been during turning.

Beckett's agony had begun to diminish and he began moaning, but his pulse was barely discernable.

At the far side of the room, Angel had already bared her arm and Darius was showing extreme skill in assembling the collecting gear. His face was deadpan but Lane could read his inner panic and along with it the boy's obvious care for Beckett. In seconds Lane exchanged places with Darius and had found Angel's vein with accustomed ease and the blood was already dripping into the collecting bag when Beckett opened his eyes and tried to sit up.

Darius put a restraining hand on his shoulder. "No, Beckett. Lay down. You need to feed again and before you say otherwise, I should warn you that if you try to avoid it I will personally knock you into next week; I think that's the phrase. So lay the fuck down and do as you're told." His voice was harsh and stern but the moisture in his eyes told of his true feelings. Beckett would have to have been dead not to notice it. He lay back against the cushion.

"I guess this is it then, this is what I am now. One of

them."

"Oh, you think so? Well let me remind you that Lane is 'one of them' and a finer more descent person I have yet to meet. You too Beckett. And the fact that you may have to take your nourishment in a different way doesn't diminish that. You are no predator, old man. Your nourishment is given freely and safely and if that is how it's to be then you are going to have to deal with it. Sooner rather than later. I know it's a shit but we're all here for you. And it may be the time to remind you that while your personal revenge has been satisfied there are others out there that need dealing with. You made a promise in Greece to Mihai, were they empty words?"

Beckett felt ashamed, realising his self pity. He swallowed hard. "Help me up, son."

Darius stopped dead as Beckett's words filtered into his consciousness. Whether it was a slip of the tongue or not, the effect on him was profound. His voice shook, "What did you call me?"

"I said, help me up, son. Because I just realised that is how I think of you. I'm sorry if it offended you. Forget it. Just help me the hell up." He struggled onto his elbow trying to propel himself from the couch.

Darius helped him up, unable to process what Beckett had said. Then he said, "No, it's OK. I … I quite like it."

"Good, just don't hug me. That would be too much."

Lane approached with a silver cup containing Angel's blood. "Are we going to have a problem, Handsome?"

Beckett shook his head and took the cup from her and drank until it was empty.

Lane nodded at him. "Good. I haven't given you all I took from her in case you need more later."

Beckett felt the normal human blood coursing through him, energising him. And in that moment came acceptance.

Lane read him and placed a hand gently on his arm. "You'll be all right. I promise."

He smiled at her and looked over to Darius and Angel. "I know that now. I'm sorry I've been such a big pain in the backside. It won't happen again."

Lane, determined to defuse the tension and emotion in the room, laughed shortly. "I doubt that, Handsome. You've always been a pain in the backside; it's not likely to change. How do you feel now?"

"Considering how I felt a moment ago, surprisingly well."

She narrowed her eyes, "Of course that …"

He interrupted her. "That begs the question, when will it happen again? Let's hope the good Doctor Bancroft is up to the job."

Lane's telephone rang, reminding Beckett that his own phone had been switched off. He switched it on an immediately it beeped, notifying him of a text message received the day before.

He read his message with a deep frown as his senses also tracked Lane's conversation.

"Patriarch, an unexpected pleasure."

Michael Rabb, born Mihai Rabinescu in Prague at the turn of the fourteenth century, the new Patriarch of the Vampire High Council was in sombre mood.

"I thought we had agreed that we were friends, Leonora, and my friends address me as Mihai, or Michael if you prefer. Lane, my dear, I need to ask you if Father Beckett is ready for service. I'm afraid things are hotting up between the Born and the Created."

Lane smiled. "Beckett," she said. "He renounced the title along with the Church."

"Hm. Possibly so, but being a priest has little to do with the Church. He'll find his way back. So, is he ready?"

Lane glanced at Beckett's concerned expression. "Yes, I believe he is."

"Good, because I had some information of concern from Greece. It may be nothing but I'm very much afraid that it isn't over. Please be ready."

Lane fell silent, reaching into the ether in an effort to fully understand the meaning of Mihai's terse warning.

"I'll contact you when I have a fuller picture. But I fear there may yet be cause for concern. Goodbye Lane." The constant burr on the line indicated that the Patriarch had hung up.

Lane put the receiver down carefully. Beckett interrupted her thoughts.

"It's from Jude Mason," he said, waving his cell phone at her. "Read it."

Lane read the digital message. "Help me, Beckett. For God's sake, help me."

CHAPTER EIGHT: THE FARMHOUSE

Unable to get a reply from Jude Mason's telephone, Beckett and Lane decided to head out to the remote farmhouse.

Lane took the B roads from Crickhowell, both of them preferring the scenic drive through the rugged vistas of the mountain region towards Pen Y Fan. The roads became mere tracks as they left the village of Cwmgwdi and Beckett began searching for the turning to the farmhouse.

"Here," said Beckett, pointing at a sign at a small turning, 'Brecon Beacons Training Centre'.

"I'm beginning to think you were right, we should have brought your heap, it's barely a track," said Lane.

They continued at a snail's pace down the stony track that was more mud than trackway. It ran through a small copse, and as they emerged at the other side, the farmhouse with its numerous outbuildings came into view.

Traditional welsh stone, it was built two hundred years previously and had been the centre of sheep farming for the two centuries in a place where not much grew and the inhospitable landscape was nurturing to only the hardy breed of welsh sheep. No livestock was in evidence as they got out of Lane's MG and as they approached the front door, it stood ajar.

"Hello!" shouted Beckett. "Hello, Mr Mason?" He pushed the door open further.

Lane put a hand on Beckett's arm. "Wait, Handsome. Use your senses, there's something very wrong here."

Beckett relaxed and focussed his heightened senses of hearing and scent. His nostril twitched as the scent of blood assailed them. He could hear no sound from within the house but there was something, a presence that rang bells of alarm in his deeper consciousness. Lane read him and nodded. "Well, done. You sense it too, though the place reeks of blood, you'd have to be dead not to smell it." She wrinkled her nose, "And it's human."

They were both on high alert as Lane leaned forwards and pushed the door wide open.

Inside, lights were burning despite it being a bright day and the room had obviously been the scene of some turmoil or other, resembling the aftermath of a natural disaster. Furniture had been overturned and the ancient welsh dresser, although still standing against the back wall, had been cleared of its china, which now lay shattered across the flagstone floor.

"What the hell, happened here?" demanded Beckett of no one in particular. "And what is that god awful stench?"

Lane concentrated her vampire senses on a scent that no human would detect. The source of which seemed to be underneath the flagstones on which they stood.

"The cellar," they said in unison. Beckett yanked open a small door to the left of the dresser and Lane moved in vampire mode and was at the foot of the wooden staircase in a fraction of a second. The cellars covered the entire footprint of the old house and one room opened up into another. The door into the adjoining room was heavily studded and was locked from the inside.

Beckett sniffed the air. "I know that smell now."

Lane nodded. "Wet dog. A *big* wet dog. Stand back Handsome, I'm stronger than you. For now."

Beckett stood aside as Lane hurled herself at the door. There was the sound of splintering wood but the door held. As she threw herself forwards a second time, Beckett kicked out against it simultaneously. Their joint force parted the huge iron bolt from the door jamb and together they moved at lightening speed into the darkened cellar. Their vampire eyes pierced the darkness, across the room to the far wall.

Heavy chains hung from high on the wall attached to

manacles. Jude Mason hung chained against the wall, his head fallen onto his bare chest which was splattered with blood and covered in deep gashes, sweat and mud. What was left of his clothing hung in tatters and a chair fallen to the side gave explanation to how this had been possible. To a human eye he appeared dead, not breathing, but Lane and Beckett simultaneously read a faint heartbeat.

"Those irons are not beyond me, but I fear we don't have the time," she said.

Beckett was already at the top of the wooden staircase and heading for the outbuildings. It may no longer be a working farm but the nature of his business meant that Jude Mason would have some serious outdoor equipment somewhere about the place.

Beckett didn't stop to be aware of the speed in which he moved, a mere shadow, a flicker of movement to human sight. The first outbuilding yielded nothing but the second, a smaller building, housed what he searched for. Propped against the inside of the door was a huge axe. He grabbed it and his shadow crossed the threshold once more as he moved with vampire speed back to the cellar. He heard Lane somewhere inside his head. *Hurry Beckett!.*

Back in the cellar he drew the axe sharply over his head and aimed with deadly accuracy at the chain just above Mason's manacled wrist. It gave with a clanking sound and as the second followed likewise, Lane caught him as he fell away from the wall. Despite his muscular build she picked him up and carried him up the staircase and into the wrecked room. She laid him on an old sofa and bent over him, gently moving the dreadlocks away from his blood smeared face.

She looked at Beckett, "Christ, Beckett, can't you sense it?"

Beckett remained stone faced but the twitch of his cheek muscles betrayed his anxiety. He ran his fingers through his hair. "He smells of wet dog. It looks as though he's been attacked by some wild animal, a wild dog maybe.

Those gouges on his chest have been made with claws."

Lane was quiet for a moment. "Not a wild animal, Handsome. Those claw marks have thumbs."

Lane had opened her mind to him and he accepted her invitation. As he read her, he took a step backwards.

"God in heaven, no. How can that be?"

Before there could be any further debate they both sensed an increase in Mason's heartbeat. It picked up speed at an alarming rate before settling into a more normal rhythm. As they watched him anxiously he began to moan quietly and toss his head from side to side. He opened his eyes and they held something that Beckett had not seen in him previously, something wild, something feral.

CHAPTER NINE: NOT PTSD

Beckett read Lane and instantly turned to the sink under the window and drew a glass of water. He returned as a shadow moves and she held the glass to the parted lips.

Jude Mason drank deep and long then lay back on the sofa. He turned to Beckett. "I'm sorry, Beckett. It's too late. I left it too late. You should leave, both of you. For everyone's sake."

Lane studied him closely, probing his mind, feeling the barrier and not wanting to push too far. There was injury there, deep in his mind and she had no intention of pushing him into crisis.

"I don't think we're in any danger. Not until night. That's so isn't it?"

Beckett raised an eyebrow. "Sorry, this is Dr Lane Dearing, we work together and I thought that she may possibly help," he said pointedly.

Jude Mason shook his head, "I'm past help, Beckett. Unless you'll do the honours with my shotgun, that is? If not, don't worry, I can manage it myself."

Lane persisted. "You chained yourself to the wall I take it. Standing on the chair while you snapped the manacles closed. I see they were rigged to self lock. No key to worry about."

Beckett frowned, once more unable to read Lane.

"Did you find your answer? You understand now what is happening to you?" she continued.

He nodded reluctantly. "Yes. The PTSD is out of control and so am I. Please, Dr Dearing, take Beckett with you and get the hell out of here. Before …"

"Before you lose control and turn on us. Before you lose yourself in the rage and the urge to kill? I sense the blood on you is your own but there is other blood too. Animal blood. I expect there may be a nearby farmer minus a sheep or two when he next goes to check his flock. Isn't that so, Mr Mason? Or may I call you, Jude?"

"You can call me whatever the hell you like, as long as it's from a distance. I'm not safe to be around. Please, both of you leave."

Images chased through Beckett's consciousness, images that gripped his heart with icy fingers. Why hadn't he seen this before? How had he missed it?

Lane sensed his thoughts as if he had spoken them aloud. "Because it hadn't developed fully until now, Handsome. Don't beat yourself up." She turned to Jude, "If what I believe is happening to you, Jude, we are going to need help."

Beckett frowned at her. PTSD was well within both of their capabilities to deal with. She shook her head. "Not PTSD Beckett. Lycanthropy."

"That could also be a side effect of PTSD," replied Beckett. "It could be the result of a hallucinogen. It's way out of civilisation up here, there could be any number of things growing out there to cause this." He turned to Jude, "I don't believe you've taken anything deliberately?"

Jude was on his feet and slavering and snarling at Beckett, his hands curled into a parody of claws. "I don't do drugs, if that's what you mean. Now get out. Get out, both of you." Suddenly he threw his head back and as rage and pain overwhelmed him he bent over clutching his stomach and screamed, although Beckett would remember it as a howl. As quickly as it had overtaken him, the spasm seemed to leave him and he pushed Lane violently to one side and ran out of the door. Beckett went to follow him, but Lane grabbed his arm and shook her head.

"This is his territory, Handsome. It won't do any good chasing him over the hills. He'll come back. He has to."

Beckett looked puzzled. "Lycanthropy? I take it you mean the psychological disorder that leaves the victim believing that he has the ability to turn into a wolf and makes him behave accordingly?"

She shook her head. "No, Beckett. I mean that he actually does become wolf. I think we both know what I'm talking about."

Beckett laughed aloud. "Jesus Lane, can you hear what you're suggesting?"

"It's not a suggestion, Handsome. If I'm not mistaken this is the real thing."

"You can't mean it. It's not possible."

"Oh really? May I remind you of what you …"

"No," he snapped, "You don't need to remind me of what I am. Thank you."

"And how is that different? Isn't it just another condition brought about by an irreversible change in DNA? A mutation? I'll bet my house on it, Handsome, he's Lycan."

"Lycan? You mean he's …"

"Yes," she said thoughtfully, "Jude Mason is a werewolf."

CHAPTER TEN: SOMETHING WILD

"A werewolf. A man who turns into a wolf on the full moon and runs around on all fours, naked and hairy, ripping people apart. I've seen Lon Chaney Junior, and I have to say I have doubts about what you are saying here, Lane."

She narrowed her eyes and reached into him. "I've seen Bela Lugosi, and Christopher Lee, but you know what, we don't sleep in coffins filled with our native soil, we don't burn up to dust in sunlight, and a crucifix won't kill us. But we exist, Beckett. Don't confuse fiction with fact, Handsome. You should know better."

"So, a werewolf who doesn't turn into a wolf? But you said he became wolf, what else could you mean by that?"

"I mean the essence of the wolf overrides the human in him and his DNA is radically changed. Maybe the full moon has an effect, maybe it doesn't. In my reckoning the moon began its cycle of full last night and he was obviously out on the rampage then. Honestly? I have no idea about this, but I know someone who does."

"Of course you do", he said dryly. "No … I'm sorry. I know that the vampire condition is caused by the virus and who knows what else is possible. I didn't mean to be arrogant; it's just that it's taken me ten years to comprehend what I have now become, what you are. Mihai, the Council, it's huge. But I understand that. Talk to me. Mickey Mouse version."

"No. Not yet. I need to understand more myself. I need to talk to the one guy who can help us to understand and maybe even help Jude. Let's go."

"Go? Just like that? Leaving him in that state, wandering around doing God knows what?"

"Do you have a better idea? He's your patient Beckett, what would you do if he presented with *any* condition you didn't have a handle on?"

"Research. Take advice."

"So we're agreed. Let's go. We know where to find him. He hasn't taken a human life yet, I would know it. We have time."

"Lane, he threatened to kill himself."

"He won't. He would have done that instead of chaining himself up last night if he was really going to do it. Are you coming or not?"

He nodded at her and moved towards the door, glancing around him, taking it in.

They travelled thirty miles in silence when Lane suddenly said, "So are you going to acknowledge what happened to you back there?"

"Sorry?"

"The way you moved, Handsome. You accessed your vampire skills and speed. You were reading me until I closed you out, though it took an effort from me. It's progressing, Beckett."

He frowned at her. "I know. I feel it. I feel more alive than ever before, stronger, and more alert. It's kinda scary."

She laughed aloud at him. "You've been up against the most dangerous and savage of our kind and you find yourself scary. You're priceless."

He ignored her laughter. "Just supposing I go along with your werewolf theory, I'm not saying I don't still believe its psychological, a side effect of PTSD, I mean the poor guy has been to hell and back in Afghanistan. Twice. Some of the things he saw and did are enough to send anyone round the bend."

"Round the bend? Very professional label. I do know some of the things, Beckett. I was inside his head as far as I dare, but there's something locked away behind a wall of pain that will need more time. Something that even he daren't remember."

"So, PTSD in fact."

She sighed. "Have it your way for now. But I warn you, Handsome, there's something wild in him. Something that will only be contained for a certain time. Who knows if the full moon will unlock it and who knows why it hasn't appeared until now. Like I said, I know someone who understands these things better than I do."

He studied her closely, trying to read her and she laughed at him as she closed him out.

Further discussion was interrupted by the instant cacophony of Lane's pager demanding her attention and a second later her cell phone and Beckett's simultaneously loudly announcing text messages. Beckett gave a 'what the hell' look as he grabbed his phone and Lane pulled the car over. She was seconds behind him in retrieving their messages. They had all originated from the same source – Helena Bancroft. And they all said the same thing. *'Come back. Now. Urgent. HB'*

"Curiouser and curiouser said Alice," murmured Beckett. "The good doctor seems a might agitated."

Lane glanced down at the antique pocket watch which she wore on a chain around her neck. Beckett had commented on it when she had first worn it in his presence. It had been created by Thomas Harland for Catherine the Great in 1750 who had presented it to Lane as a Thank You. She had always refused to tell him what she had done to deserve her thanks and Beckett had decided that it was probably best if he didn't know.

"Send her a text and tell her we'll be there in twenty minutes."

Beckett made a deliberate parody of tightening his seat belt before keying in the message.

"Do you think she'll manage it? I mean, she was Greg Randall's assistant."

Lane nodded at him. "It's my belief that she's got what it takes. He kept her down because of his ego. She took

61

the post with him when her own research grant ran out. Her speciality is actually genetics and I understand she's quite brilliant."

Beckett fell silent, contemplating just how much her brilliance would impact on him and hoping Lane hadn't overstated it.

Several minutes later they pulled up outside the Sanctuary and Lane was swiping her entry card into the digital lock on the lab, both sensing the agitation coming from Helena.

"Thank God," she exclaimed as they entered the room.

"Where's the fire, Doc?" said Beckett in an effort to diffuse the anxiety in the atmosphere.

Helena ignored his effort. "It's not a virus!"

"What do you mean?" demanded Lane.

"It isn't a virus. It looks like a virus, it behaves like a virus but it isn't a virus. And before you ask me what the hell it is, I have no idea. Yet. And Beckett, I need you over here, now. I need blood."

Beckett laughed harshly at the irony of her words. "So what's the panic? It sounds as if we've taken a step backwards."

Helena shook her head, "That's not it. There's something alarming happening to the blood samples. At first it seemed as though the vampire cells were causing damaged human cells to regenerate, but now … now it seems as though the vampire cells are actually killing off the human cells. Right now, I have no idea what that means. But …"

"But that's not good, right Doc?" said Beckett.

Helena was already drawing blood from Beckett's arm. "It seems to be a geometric progression. Honestly? I have no idea how fast this thing will take over every cell in your body, there is some reason why you're different Beckett and it has to do with the anti bodies from Randall's treatment. I'll call you as soon as I have a better idea."

Effectively dismissed, as Helena already had one eye

glued to her microscope and was already oblivious to their presence, they left. Lane put a hand on Beckett's arm. "It may not be as bad as she made it sound."

He read her, and saw past the guilt she was harbouring as it had been Lane that had pumped the anti virus into him.

"Don't feel like that," he said. "You saved my life or my human life anyway. You did what you did for me, and I appreciate it."

Lane relaxed as she acknowledged his intrusion into her mind. "I told you that when the time came you'd find it easy."

CHAPTER ELEVEN: OUTSIDE HELP

Lane sat deep in thought then suddenly lifted the telephone and dialled. It rang at the other end for several minutes and she was about to replace the receiver when a familiar voice at the other end stopped her.

"Hello. Jo speaking."

"Hello Jo, it's Lane Dearing. It's been a long time," said Lane fondly.

"Lane. It's good to hear you. It's been close to ten years. Is this a catch up call or is this more serious?"

Jo Timberwolf was nothing if not to the point. His craggy features broke into a smile at the thought of Lane, sending a sparkle into the silver grey eyes that were reflected in his long silver hair perpetually tied casually in a long pony tail at the nape of his neck with leather thongs and turquoise beads. His tanned and leathery face was ageless and contained deep wisdom in every wrinkle. She felt as though she had known him forever, his voice was soft and reassuring and Lane couldn't remember a time when she had heard him raise his voice in anger. He was a fifth generation shaman living and working on a Navajo reservation in Arizona, loved by his people and respected by the elders of his own tribe and those of neighbouring reservations.

"You got me, Jo. I'm ashamed to say I'm calling because I need you. I'll cut right to it. I believe we have a Skinwalker." She told him all she knew about Jude Mason and her thoughts on what was happening to him. "Dare I hope you can come and help?"

Jo was silent for a moment then he said quietly, "If you are asking me to help it is because the Ancient Ones have spoken. Of course I will help. I can be there tomorrow morning."

Lane breathed a sigh of relief, "Thank you Jo. I'll have someone meet you and bring you here. Of course I'll reimburse you for your journey."

"No need Lane. When the Ancient Ones task me, I have no need for payment. Besides, I'm overdue a vacation."

"With all due respect to the Ancient Ones, Jo, there will be a ticket waiting for you at the desk at Sky Harbour International in Phoenix and my friend Darius will meet you at Heathrow. I'm grateful."

"So long, Lane. See you tomorrow."

She put down the telephone more hopeful than before the call. If Jude Mason was indeed Lycan then Jo Timberwolf was the only hope she had of the situation not ending badly. She had witnessed him performing several of the Navajo ceremonies including those dealing with Skinwalkers. She knew that the term Skinwalker had originally referred to Navajo witches that had broken taboo, usually by killing a family member before performing The Witchery Way ceremony, creating evil and wreaking havoc. They were associated with wearing the pelts of animals whose form they wished to take. More recently however, mainly due to popular fiction and the movie screen, Skinwalker was a term given to werewolves, or people that could shape shift into any animal they chose. If there was anyone that would be able to free Jude Mason it was Jo Timberwolf.

She was more relaxed when Darius stuck his head around her door. "Got a minute?"

"You're here late, come on in. Drink?"

Darius shook his head, "No thanks. I just wanted a talk that's all." He still wore the Gothic frock coat and high necked, frilled dress shirt with black jeans and high black boots. His shoulder length hair was wavy and reflected the shades of a raven's wing in the lamplight. Not for the first time, Lane acknowledged that he was beautiful. But he was clearly uneasy.

She frowned, entering his head and understanding his concerns immediately. She gave no sign of her intrusion to him. "Sounds serious," she said. "Maybe *I* need a drink."

She moved casually to the sideboard and poured whisky into a crystal glass that had once adorned the table of Louis the fourteenth. She held up the matching decanter. "Sure? You look like you need one."

Darius caved, he could never refuse Lane anything. "A small one then, thanks."

Lane smiled and poured another glass. She handed it to him. "Darius, for God's sake sit down. You're making me nervous. What's on your mind?"

"It's me. I'm doing nothing useful. I decided to stay here and work with you and Beckett but I'm doing nothing of any importance. You know I want to be out there, at the sharp end, no pun intended. I'm …"

Lane interrupted him. "You're valuable, that's what you are. I know it seems as though you're doing the job of a glorified messenger and general help but the truth is sweetheart, none of us is at the sharp end as you put it, not at the moment, though that's about to change. And pardon me for mentioning it, but I recall that if it wasn't for you we'd be short one Beckett right now."

Darius flushed, he knew Lane would have answers that would make him feel foolish without intending to.

"I just need to be out there, hunting them down and getting rid."

Lane narrowed her eyes as she sipped the old whisky. "Sounds to me like you're still angry, Darius. You wanted to be the one to put an end to Andrei and that opportunity presented itself to someone else. You can kill a thousand rogue vampires and you'll still feel the same. You need to get over it if you are ever going to be detached enough to do the job without putting everyone else in jeopardy."

He hadn't expected her to turn his need into something that sounded selfish and yet at the core of her words he recognised a truth. He sighed.

"I didn't mean to diminish what you did in Greece or subsequently, but you have major work to do in future. I know it. It just isn't that time yet," said Lane, her voice brimming with admiration and compassion.

"You just said that things were about to change, what do you know?"

"I had a call from Mihai. He said we might be needed soon, he was getting more information." She was careful not to mention Greece in his already frustrated mood. "And we have someone close to home in deep trouble."

"Oh. Who?"

"A patient of Beckett's. Name's Jude Mason and in the next few days he will live or die depending on the result of a visit from an old friend of mine, Joseph Timberwolf." She continued to explain the situation. "He's arriving tomorrow from Arizona and I want you go and meet him and bring him to the Sanctuary. Take great care of him, he's very special."

Darius nodded. "Consider it done. I hadn't expected us to branch out into werewolves I have to admit."

"Well, he's Beckett's patient. And if he's not helped or at least controlled who knows what may happen. We've still to get to the bottom of how he came to be infected.

The word 'infected' triggered his thought process and he said, "Maybe Dr Bancroft can help?"

"Yes, I'd thought of that but first of all his problem needs a more spiritual approach. Helena can take a look at him after Jo's done his stuff. I don't know where this may lead Darius, but I should warn you it could get ugly."

"Is there any truth in the myths? You know, silver bullets? Full moon etcetera."

"I think that silver may have an effect on him. Just like us. As for the full moon, Jo will be able to fill us in on the details of the condition. I do know that he doesn't change body shape and run around on all fours. At least I don't believe so. His facial hair and fingernails are subject to accelerated growth and his mouth and teeth undergo significant changes. He becomes a beast in every other sense of the word. Savage and hungry. At the moment he hasn't taken a human life but if it isn't dealt with, it will only be a matter of time."

"Then you can count on me. Thanks, Lane. For listening."

She smiled fondly at him. "My pleasure. Always. By the way, do you know where Beckett went? I didn't see or feel him leave but he's definitely not around. I could do with talking to him."

Darius shook his head. "Can't say. Though Angel did say she saw him leave and said cheerio but he didn't answer her, she said he seemed preoccupied."

Lane frowned. The last thing they needed right then was for Beckett to be off his game. Or worse.

CHAPTER TWELVE: LYCAN

Lane was concerned for Beckett. He was fragile and soon he would need to feed. It was against her ethics but she felt deep within her bones that she needed to find him. Overlooking a close friend was repugnant to her but needs must. More than her needing to find Beckett she sensed it was he that needed to find himself.

She closed her eyes and shut down her conscious mind, reaching out across the ether, searching.

Five miles away in the centre of Abergavenny she found him. His surroundings were steeped in sacred energy and Beckett was deep in a meditative state. She smiled. Beckett had gone to church.

The Priory Church of St Mary had often been called the Westminster Abbey of Wales, due to its size and the high status monuments, sarcophagi and tombs it contained. Lane hesitated outside the church sensing Beckett's contemplations. He was looking for answers, poor sod. He knew as well as she, that answers are never found outside; the truth comes from inside the heart. He had discovered that in Greece, and almost got a handle on his returning faith, but recent events had knocked that out of him and he was floundering again.

She entered through the ancient doorway and the sense of peace within the Priory Church calmed her momentarily, coming as it did from centuries of quiet worship from countless souls. As she trod softly down the central isle she couldn't help but admire the gothic arches and columns and the stunningly beautiful gothic window above the altar.

Beckett was seated to the left of the isle three rows from the front pew and even though she approached in silence he sensed her.

She sat next to him but didn't speak. After several minutes, still with closed eyes, he murmured, "I wondered how long it would take you."

"You okay, Handsome?"

"Oh, I guess I will be. You know me."

She smiled, "Yes, sadly I do. You're a lost cause if ever I saw one. There is truly no hope."

He didn't turn to her, focussing his eyes on the exquisitely carved statue of Christ on the cross. "Do you believe in God, Legs? I mean really believe."

She didn't hesitate, "Yes, I do. Otherwise I couldn't do what I do and live with it. Do I believe in a human man who claims infallibility because he's been elected by a bunch of other old men, no. Do I believe the doctrines and dogmas that often cause more suffering than they are meant to relieve, then no. Do I believe that we are all the product of a supreme creator, then yes. There is too much symmetry and perfection in the universe for it to have been the result of a cosmic belch. Do I believe that there is only one way to approach that Creator? No. I know you found your way back in Greece when you prayed for Katerini. I saw it. But you let it go, Beckett. Mihai said you would find your way back. You're just stubborn, that's all. I sensed that it was important to him."

She read him and felt his inner yearning for what he had once been but in a new way, his way.

"Being a priest has little to do with the Church, Handsome; it's helping a soul to heal itself. In whatever way each individual soul needs. Especially at the time that the soul leaves the body to return to the source. You did that for Kat. And I hope that if the need arises, you will do it for me."

He turned to look directly at her, placing his hand gently on her cheek, "I will never allow that need to arise."

She was shocked at the intensity in his eyes and there was something else, something that made her heart leap.

She dismissed it abruptly.

"Good. That much we agree on. So now will you come back with me? We need to talk about your Jude Mason. In fact I want to go back out to the farm."

He laughed, "Now? Can't a man, well, vampire find a moments peace with God?"

"Pack him up where he belongs, inside, and haul him out of here with you."

"Some would call that blasphemy," he joked.

"Then they would be fools," she replied quietly, taking in every contour of his face, his intense eyes that always seemed to harbour sadness. She was shaken by the feelings that had briefly ignited in her. Feelings that could have no future.

They discussed the arrival of Jo Timberwolf and Lane told him of her talk with Darius and the boy's frustration. Beckett's eyes found a twinkle at the mention of Darius. He understood the driving need for revenge in the boy; he was too familiar with it. And in Greece, Darius had been robbed of the chance to taste the revenge as Andrei had been killed by one of his own; Santorini, aka Greg Randall.

"He'll be fine. Just don't let him know that there is still a problem in Greece. Has Mihai clarified that?"

Lane shook her head. "No. I'm still waiting for him to get back to me. Whatever it is, he's shielding it from me. And that isn't good. Mihai has always been open with me and as Proconsul of the council he should keep me in the loop. We have a choice, Beckett. We stay and deal with what's happening to Jude Mason, help Jo in whatever way we can and then go out to Greece and see for ourselves what's happening there. Or we can just go right now."

"No choice in fact. That feeling is getting very familiar. I've been thinking about Jude. Perhaps I have been stubborn about the PTSD diagnosis, but I'm willing to listen. What do you know?"

"Not as much as I'd like, that's why Jo is on his way here from Arizona. I can tell you that stories of lycanthropy, werewolves if you like, go back to Ovid who wrote '*In vain he attempted to speak, his jaws were spattered with blood and he thirsted for blood as he raged among flocks and panted for slaughter. His vesture was changed into hair, his limbs became crooked – a wolf. He retains much of his ancient expression, his countenance rabid, his eyes glitter savagely, the picture of fury'*. Or words to that effect. Sound familiar? Sounds like Jude Mason to me. And it wasn't just Ovid; Pliny had his say as well. Legends leave their trail throughout history from Ancient Greece to almost present day and throughout nearly every culture. In France they are known as Loup Garoux and believed by all classes. And it goes without saying how Hollywood has tapped into the subconscious acceptance of the beast."

"Okay, so Jude is a werewolf or what did you call him?"

"Lycan. That's the latest term among psychiatrists as well as popular fiction."

"So Jude is Lycan. How did that happen? Because to my knowledge, apart from the trauma of being SAS in Afghanistan, he has no prior psychological problems."

"Then we start there. In Afghanistan."

"I warn you, he won't discuss it."

"Then I'll have to go in and see his memories for myself. Assuming we can get hold of him that is."

"Then we'd better go get him, hadn't we. My car this time." Beckett was ahead of her leaving the Priory Church and in vampire speed was already waiting for her at the wheel of his beaten up four by four. Lane rolled her eyes but conceded the discomfort was better than damage to her precious MG.

CHAPTER THIRTEEN: THE HARD WAY.

Jude Mason's farmhouse stood in darkness. Its shadow cast by the full moon loomed across the cobbled courtyard. Lane and Beckett were at the door simultaneously.

"He's been busy," muttered Beckett as he took in the heavily barred door and windows.

Lane was listening to her accentuated hearing and before she could alert Beckett, he too had heard the rage and torment originating from the basement in the sealed building.

"I hear him," he said in reply to her unspoken question. "You go left."

They separated and went in opposite directions checking the building for possible entry points. Jude had done a good job. Entry would have to be forced and dramatic. Beckett stood aside, not because Lane was stronger than he was but more because he knew how much she enjoyed breaking and entering.

The door and the wooden barrier behind it splintered as she hit it hard with both feet and they were inside in a heartbeat and heading towards the small door at the side of the old dresser.

At the top of the stairs they both hesitated, connecting with what was happening in the room below. They sensed Jude Mason chained to the wall once again, in agony and torment. The howling had stopped as he sensed them above him. Chains were clanking against stone wall and there was a steady low growl as he listened and sniffed and waited.

Beckett put a restraining hand on Lane and shook his

head, pointing back to the room upstairs. She understood immediately, to confront Jude in his current state would end in only one way. Someone was going to get hurt. They needed to wait until the pain, rage and blood lust had passed and he was himself once again. There would be no helping him in his present state. The beast within him had to be quiescent.

As they ascended the wooden staircase Beckett once again signalled to Lane and this time she was way ahead of him. They weren't alone.

They sensed female and they sensed anxiety. Lane moved first, catlike and silent, Becket was a second behind her. The female presence was immediately behind the door, and holding her breath. Beckett understood Lane's warning glance and nodded his understanding.

Lane pushed the door open violently, taking the girl by surprise. Beckett's arm shot out faster than she was able to track it. He held her firmly but not wishing to harm her.

"It's all right," said Lane. "We don't want to hurt you. We are here to help him."

Sabine's eyes were wide and she was trembling. "Who are you? What have you done with him?"

She kept her eyes on Beckett and he took her lead. "My name is Beckett and this is Dr. Lane Dearing. We are here to help Jude Mason. What are you doing here?"

Sabine's eyes darkened and she appeared to relax a little. Beckett persisted. "Is that his name? Jude mason? Are you friends of his?"

Lane connected with her sudden intentions as she acted on them. As Sabine turned and bolted for the door, Lane launched herself into the air and jumped clean over the girl's head, landing in the doorway facing her. Sabine stopped dead in her tracks, her face ashen.

"What *are* you?"

Lane raised a hand to stop the questions, her face severe. Beckett interrupted her.

"What we are doesn't matter. It's what Jude Mason is

that's our current concern and from the look of you, you're worried about him too. Why don't you come and sit down and tell us about it?"

Sabine started as the clanging of chains in the cellar accompanied a spine chilling roar.

Sabine began to tremble. "I … I don't know him. I only saw him yesterday … in the forest. He ran away before I could talk to him. I only wanted to help him."

"With respect," said Lane, "I don't think there's a whole lot you can do for him."

"I can be his friend. He needs a friend. I saw what happens to him. I know what is happening to him."

"You know?" queried Beckett.

Sabine nodded but said nothing.

Lane continued her frosty interrogation. "I suggest you tell us what you think you know."

Beckett frowned at her. *Good cop, bad cop? Really?*

He put a hand on her arm and she flinched, he took it away slowly. "We won't hurt you. I promise. Please tell us what you know. It may help him."

Sabine sat down heavily on the old sofa and seemed to sag in the middle. When she looked up at Beckett there were tears on her cheek. He didn't touch her, not wanting to spook her again. Lane relaxed as she connected with the girl's thoughts, she was a tainted innocent.

Jude Mason continued to rage and howl downstairs in the cellar, each howl of torment made Sabine blanche a shade paler. "Can't you do anything? Please, help him."

"Not while he's in this phase. We'll have to wait until it passes. Then we'll take him back with us, someone is coming who can help him better than either of us."

Sabine shook her head, "No, he needs to know that someone cares. Right now, while the rage is on him, he needs to know someone cares." She bolted for the stairs taking both Lane and Beckett by surprise. Lane launched herself forwards but Sabine had slammed the door behind her and was taking the stairs two at a time.

"Damn!" shouted Lane, hurling the door open and following Sabine with lightening speed. She stopped at the bottom of the stairs, arm outstretched to Sabine, her eyes pleading with girl to step back from Jude who had momentarily ceased howling and raging and yanking on his chains. His face looked leaner, darker somehow, his cheeks covered in coarse hair, his mouth distorted, his teeth the teeth of a rabid dog. But his eyes held an uncanny curiosity. He had seen the girl in the woods, and she had seemed unafraid, speaking to him with compassion. Now she stood in front of him, reaching out to him. A low growl came from his foaming lips and he let his head fall forwards onto his chest.

Sabine approached him slowly. "I saw you in the forest. I know what is happening to you. I know the pain you are in. There are people here that want to help you. Please. Please let them help you."

Before either could react, Sabine stepped directly in front of Jude and laid a hand on the course hair covering his cheek and gently stroked his face.

The low growl continued and then Jude threw back his head and let out a soul chilling howl before letting his head fall again and he began to weep.

Lane approached him slowly as Sabine moved in front of him protectively, her eyes flashing a warning.

"I told you, we're not here to hurt him. But if we're going to be able to help him, it won't be here. He needs to come back with us." Lane glanced down at her watch, "Where very soon there will be an expert on hand to help try and put things right for him."

Sabine narrowed her eyes, "I don't know who or what you are, but know this, I will do whatever I can to protect him, and I realise that may involve my life. I didn't step up last time and it cost someone dear to me his life. I have had to live with that for five years. I have another chance to be able to look in the mirror. And just so you know … where he goes, I go."

Beckett smiled at her, his eyes holding a sparkle long since lost. There was something of Grace about the girl, maybe the determined chin or something in her eyes.

"You did say you only met him yesterday, right?"

Sabine shook her head. "No. I never really met him."

Jude stood upright suddenly and yanked on the manacles holding him chained to the wall. His eyes no longer contained the wild look of moments earlier as he directed his gaze to Beckett. "If you really want to help, you can get me off this wall, get the hell out and leave me with my shotgun."

"Yeah, we can do that," said Beckett without emotion, "Or you could just do it the hard way, come back with us and let us at least try. Or maybe you weren't really the stuff Special Forces are made of. Maybe deep down you don't have what it takes to fight this thing."

Jude glared at him, small flecks of foam appearing at the corner of his mouth, the low growl starting deep in his throat, his eyes once again feral. "You have no idea," he growled.

"Actually my friend, I have every idea. Really. And if you're serious about the shotgun then go ahead but then you'll never really know just what you're made of."

"I know what I'm made of. In Afghanistan …"

"Yeah yeah, Special Forces, Afghanistan, I get it. But that's not here, not now, not this."

"Don't!" shouted Sabine. "Leave him alone! Can't you see how he's suffering? You're not human!"

"'Aint that the truth," muttered Beckett.

"Enough, all of you," Lane interrupted. She strode forwards something glinting in her hand and with only Beckett able to track her movements she inserted the hypodermic needle into Jude's neck and stood back as the manacles bore his weight when he fell forwards. "Let's get him into the car, minus the shotgun. And yes, you can come too," she said to Sabine. "You seem to be able to calm him and he's going to be extremely pissed when he wakes up. Then maybe you can get your story off your chest."

Sabine frowned at Lane and then suddenly broke into a smile. "You really aren't going to kill him are you?"

"No, honey, we're not going to kill him." *Unless we have to,* she thought.

Beckett read her and acknowledged her unspoken thought. *We have to make damn sure we don't have to.*

Jude sat slumped against Sabine in the back of Beckett's rust bucket. She had her arm around him protectively as he lay motionless.

"What did you give him?" she asked Lane.

"Ketamine. It's a horse tranquiliser, and I figured given his rage and strength it was going to take it."

"I know what Ketamine is, but did you have to cosh him that hard?"

"You saw him, what do you suggest?"

Sabine shook her head dislodging the tear at the corner of her eye. She looked away, concentrating on the scene passing by.

"Where are you taking him?"

Beckett glanced at Lane. *Tell her. She's going to find out anyway.*

Lane considered a moment. "We're going to a place called The Sanctuary, it's in Newport and it's a place that vampires can go to if they get into trouble with those of our kind that have no scruples about killing humans. Or to feed ethically from blood given freely by donors. We have the facilities there we are going to need for Jude."

She waited for the onslaught from Sabine but it didn't come.

"So that's what you are? Vampires?"

"That's what we are."

"My family is descended from Abraham Wood the first Romany to come to this country, we are Rom, and we know of these things. And Varcolac, or Werewolf. There is no cure. ... Only death."

"You said someone very close to you," prompted Beckett.

Sabine was quiet, her thoughts dark as Beckett read them. "My young brother, Abram. I loved him very much. He became sick, the victim of Varcolac. We weren't able to stop him, and when a small child disappeared from our community, they took things into their own hands and killed him. But it wasn't him. I know it wasn't him, because I know who really took the child. It was too late to save Abram, but I could have told what I know. My father is very weak, he's been that way since Abram, and they said they would take his life if I spoke out. The leader of our community was also Varcolac and it was he that made my brother that way and it was he that took the child. Everyone feared him. It is why we left the community and now we travel alone."

"We?"

"My father, my uncle and my cousins. We just want to live in peace, and it is in this place that we seem to be able to come close to that."

Daylight was fingering its way to Beckett's retinas and he squinted against it.

Lane noticed immediately. "Pull over, Beckett, I'll drive. Where the hell are your contacts?"

"I just hate poking my finger in my eyes every goddamn morning. Okay, okay, I'll pull over."

He stopped his car and got out, slamming the door as Lane slid her slender frame into the driver's seat. He climbed into the passenger seat and reached into the glove compartment for his sunglasses.

Sabine claimed his attention, "So … you can be in the sun?"

"Yes. Don't worry, we're not about to turn into the contents of an egg timer. It's more than uncomfortable even with the sun block but my eyes are sore because my retinas react badly to ultra violet light."

Sabine seemed to be considering the information.

Eventually, she relaxed into her seat and said to Beckett, "Then I think maybe you can help him."

CHAPTER FOURTEEN: DARK MEMORIES

Sabine had protested loudly as Beckett and Lane strapped Jude to a table with huge leather straps at intervals up his body. His feet and wrists were strapped to the edge of the table and there was a heavy strap around his head. Lane had responded with impatience.

"Look, if you are going to stay here, and I recommend it, you are going to have keep out of our way. Yes, it looks horrible, but really, do you want him rampaging around the place until some hot shot copper shoots him? You want that?"

Sabine calmed and shook her head. She had seen Abram gunned down when at the height of the rage cycle. She owed it to him to let them do what they thought necessary for Jude.

"I'm sorry. But it's what will happen if we don't contain him," continued Lane. "He's going to be hard to control when he wakes and I don't particularly want to become meatloaf. Look maybe it would be better if you went with Angel, have a coffee or something but just don't leave."

Sabine left in search of Angel, annoyed at being sent out of the room but beginning to believe in Lane.

Jude began to moan. Beckett and Lane were instantly at his side. Lane looked anxiously at her watch. "Jo will be here very soon, I don't want to drug him again unless I have to. He'll be out for hours."

"I thought he'd be out longer than this," replied Beckett.

Lane nodded. "Yes, I know."

Jude spoke suddenly, "It's over for now. I can feel it."

He opened his eyes and tried to move his head. "I can break these straps but I'd rather you just removed them."

Beckett read him. He started to unbuckle the strap around Jude's head.

"What the hell are you doing, Handsome?"

"It's all right. He's going nowhere."

"Thanks," said Jude. "I'm afraid you haven't seen me at my best."

Beckett laughed harshly. "Depends which way you look at it." He released the remainder of the restraints and Jude sat up. He looked down at his muscular bare chest and gingerly touched the wounds along the length of his ribs. He put his hand to his face. "Don't suppose you've got a spare razor?"

Then as suddenly as he'd awoken, he slammed his fist into the table. "I don't know what the hell you think you can do. You've seen what I am for God's sake. There is only one thing that will stop me from killing someone."

His train of thought progressed and he stood up abruptly. "There was a girl ... I remember a girl. Where is she?" he demanded.

Again Beckett was tracking his thoughts. "It's okay. You didn't harm her, she's here. Wouldn't leave you actually. I'm afraid she doesn't quite trust us. How about you Jude? Do you trust us?"

"I don't know yet. Do I have a choice?"

"Not in my opinion," said Lane flatly. "Shotguns can be rather messy. Think of the poor sod that finds you. It won't be pretty."

Jude's eyes displayed his curiosity. "And just what do you think you can do?"

Lane sat in a club chair in the corner of the room, pulled out a packet of cigarettes and lit one, flicking her gold lighter into life with what seemed nothing more than thought.

He became irritable and Beckett moved in front of Lane, ready for any sign of an attack.

Jude arched an eyebrow at Beckett as he transferred his attention from Lane. "Sorry. Look, let's not mess about. Tell me if you think it's hopeless and I *will* take care of the situation myself. Regardless of the mess."

Voices on the street outside alerted Lane and Beckett to the arrival of Darius and his charge.

Beckett looked directly into Jude's eyes. "I promise that if nothing can be done, I'll help you. No need for a mess."

Jude nodded. "I believe you. So what now?"

Lane was about to speak but Beckett pre-empted her.

"Now, I want you to allow me access to your mind. It will help to know how this happened to you. I know, I know, you can't remember what happened, but that's the point. You've locked it away so you don't have to deal with it, but if you'll allow me, I can retrieve that information and help you deal with it."

"You know, when you speak like that I can almost believe you're just a therapist, Beckett, not a bloody vampire."

"Maybe it's because I'm a bloody vampire that makes you trust me. I sense you do."

Lane stood, clicking her nails together as she smoked. "I'll be outside." *You sure you can do this, Beckett?* she thought.

I can do this, Legs. I need to do this.

Lane nodded her understanding and left.

Outside in the hall, Darius was introducing Angel and Sabine to Jo Timberwolf. They all looked up at Lane's approach. Jo moved forwards, his leathery face creased in a smile that reached his silver eyes. He pulled Lane to him and embraced her fondly.

"Hello, Lane. I was about to say you haven't aged a day, but that would be somewhat lacking in taste. You do look good though. And this …" he gestured around him. "This must be your brainchild. You told me about how you wanted to create a sanctuary for innocents caught up in the strange world of yours. That was ten years ago, and now I see you have achieved your goal. It's impressive. As is this young man. We have had a very interesting journey."

Lane kissed the old Navajo on his cheek. "Jo. This is so good of you. I don't know enough to do this without you. Skinwalkers are unfamiliar territory."

He nodded, his expression serious. "When can I see him?"

"Soon. My friend and partner, Beckett, is with him at the moment, trying to determine the source of the problem. We believe it was in Afghanistan."

If he was surprised, Jo didn't show it. "Go on."

"He's ex Special Forces. He came home from a deployment in Afghanistan recently. Not the first time he'd been there. Well, he went to pieces and was discharged from the service on health grounds, Beckett has been treating him for Post Traumatic Stress Disorder, but we've come to understand the true diagnosis. Although 'understand' isn't strictly the right word."

Jo nodded thoughtfully. "The behaviour of Skinwalker is close to the symptoms of what you call PTSD. An easy mistake. Your friend, is he like you?"

Lane nodded, "Yes, I'm rather afraid he is."

"There is more in your voice than friendship, Lane. You deny your true feelings, I think."

Lane glanced uncomfortably at Darius and steered Jo away. "He's ... vulnerable. Right now, he's accessing Jude Mason's locked away memories and pain, searching for the source. I believe it's important."

"The Ancient Ones know what is important and only if they decide to protect this man will they allow your partner to access this part of his mind. Come," he said, linking his arm through Lane's, "tell me about him."

There had been little resistance to Beckett's probing and searching through layers of memory and experience, pleasure and pain accumulating into what had made the man Jude Mason. He came suddenly to a barrier, an effective wall of protection that took him several minutes to breach. He took in a sharp breath as the surge of horror and pain washed over him. He steadied himself and pushed forwards.

* * *

It was dark and Sergeant Jude Mason was floating towards the ground. He was parachuting into the White Mountain region of Afghanistan and could see the rough terrain in an eerie green light. Night vision goggles gave him sight of the rugged cliffs and barren landscape littered with valleys of course gravel and boulders. The mountain tops shone white in the green hue, a legacy of the harsh snows of the Afghan winter. The sight was familiar; once again the regiment had been deployed to clear the now infamous caves of Tora Bora.

Since Bin Laden's demise the Al Quaida hierarchy had fallen apart and the footsoldiers were disorganised and in disarray. One by one and in small groups they had travelled back to the region only six kilometres north of the Pakistan border to inhabit the caves once again.

Contrary to popular belief that the caves of Tora Bora were a huge underground complex of passages, bunkers and weapons storage units they were in fact a labyrinth of natural caves and connecting tunnels in the jagged cliff faces. Intelligence and counter intelligence had been confusing but he had been there back in 2001 when the much written about 'Battle for Tora Bora' had taken place. A joint mission from Special Forces from both the United Kingdom and the States had resulted in the routing of the Taliban from the area and the near miss on Bin Laden.

The ground connected with his boots and he rolled away from the impact, dragging the parachute towards him. He hit the release button and took the ground running low. The others of Alpha Two Four were approaching and wordlessly they began the hazardous climb to the first cave entrance.

Insurgents and Taliban had retaken the caves in 2007 but had rapidly been sent packing by others like him. This mission would be quickly over and he would be redeployed again. Confirmed intelligence out of Pakistan had shown a regrouping of Taliban and new insurgents once again in the cave complex in the White Mountains. This time it was solely a Regiment mission. He had an illogical sense of foreboding contrary to the nature of the job or him.

Ordered by a series of gestures from Lieutenant Ben Baxter they converged on the cave entrance now littered with evidence of previous occupation. Inside the first passage a faint glimmer of a distant light fired an alarm in his chest. They were on.

More gestures from Baxter caused them to separate where the tunnel diverged, effectively dividing them. He and Carl Thomas went left, Baxter and Dave Burton right. As they took the tunnel slowly and soundlessly the glimmer of light became brighter and low voices speaking in various dialects could be plainly heard.

Jude's finger's tightened around the trigger of his MP5 sub machine gun, comforted by its presence against his body. Thomas was striding ahead; stupid bugger was constantly taking risks. Problem was it was more than just *his* life at stake; he had to toe the team line. 'In theatre' was no place for a maverick. When they got back Baxter was going to insist the colonel do something.

Without warning Thomas had pulled the pin on a tear gas grenade. That wasn't in the programme, and the consequence of breathing in the gas in the confinement of the tunnels was likely to cause damage to more than the Taliban. He grabbed at his gas mask and his sudden movement caused Thomas to spin around.

Jude gestured angrily at him and was answered with a casual wave of the hand before a shrug as he put the pin back into the grenade and stowed it back on his belt. As he turned into the tunnel again Thomas's foot connected with a stray rock and he slipped. He grabbed at the rock face to steady himself but the noise had been enough. The voices stopped suddenly and there was a tell tale crunch of boots on the shale floor of the tunnel which had suddenly opened out into another cave.

The fire fight was sudden and over quickly, the Taliban weapons and skill unequal to those of the Regiment. The familiar sound of running footsteps announced the arrival of Baxter and Burton at the same time as lights in another tunnel to the rear of the cave told them more insurgents and Taliban would be on them in moments.

There was a sharp pain in his chest accompanied by intense heat and a feeling of light headedness. He looked down at the place just to the left of his heart where the bullet had penetrated at the edge of his vest. He was shot.

Blackness engulfed him and when he was next aware of his surroundings the bodies of the other three lay in a bloodied heap with entrails seeping into the cave floor. He struggled to his feet, thinking fast, assessing his options. Three bearded insurgents, dirtied and bloodied from weeks in the caves and the gun battle that had just taken place, loomed in front of him. His instinctive grab for his gun proved futile. The insurgent in the centre of the group laughed, showing blackened teeth through the dark stubble, and waved his gun at him. He threw it to the floor behind them and in a moment they were transforming.

Coarse hair was sprouting along the line of their cheekbones and covering their cheeks. Their eyes took on a wild look and somehow seemed to be changing colour, becoming almost luminescent. Their jaw line seemed to be pulsating and as he stood transfixed their teeth became savage points in slavering jaws.

They were on him in a heartbeat and the one that had taken his gun was ripping into his chest with teeth and claws and as consciousness threatened to leave him again he threw his arm up in defence and the brutal jaws that had been aiming at his throat connected with the fleshy part of his upper arm. It was all he needed to roll out of range and grab his abandoned weapon. The first werewolf got the first bullet between the eyes, the second and third right over the heart. Others were reaching the scene and they too were transforming before him.

The bloody Taliban were breeding werewolves as weapons. An army of werewolves would soon come from the few in front of him.

The grenade was in his hand before he had conscious thought and as he hurled it into their mist he leaped into the tunnel one second before the explosion ripped through the cave.

Blood was pouring down his arm and from the bullet wound in his chest but Jude Mason was on his way out of the tunnels and into the reassuring cover of darkness before the rest of the insurgents could gather their wits.

He didn't stop until he was way out of range and then only to tie a tight bandage ripped from the bottom of his jacket. The bullet had passed through him on his left side and although he had originally lost a lot of blood, the bleeding had almost stopped. The severe arm wound was the result of him losing a mouthful of flesh to the slavering jaws of the werewolf.

* * *

There was a tight feeling and a sharp pain in Beckett's chest and as he opened his eyes to face Jude, he saw that explanations would be unnecessary. Jude had been a part of the whole process and had relived every moment with him. Beads of perspiration stood out on his brow and he was visibly shaking.

CHAPTER FIFTEEN: SHAMAN

"Bastards! A goddamn army of werewolves!" Jude spat. "Doesn't help me now though does it?"

Beckett was shaken by the experience and could feel Lane in his head, steadying him, supporting him. *Okay Handsome. You did great. Now walk away from him, sit in the chair in the corner and get yourself together.* Her voice was as audible as if she had spoken from within the room. He obeyed readily.

"It may not have any relevance to us but to Jo it may mean a whole lot," Beckett said to Jude.

On cue the door opened and Lane entered with Jo at her side. The gnarled old shaman held out a hand to Jude and nodded at him. "Wolf is strong in you. You have been bitten by one who was Alpha and ruthless. It is well the Ancient Ones have brought me to you. But you have to open your mind and your heart to the healing that will take place and you must banish the thoughts of taking your own life for that darkens your soul and makes it vulnerable to wolf. I have hopes for your recovery because there is one who prays constantly for your soul."

He patted the back of Jude's hand and gently released it. He turned to Lane, "I believe we should begin right away. There are two ceremonies that will take place to banish wolf from his soul, known to my people as Anaa'ji, The Enemy Way and Hozhooji, the Blessing Way. These ceremonies cleanse and heal the soul and allow it to continue its earthly journey. The Holy Ones will be invited to come and play their part and if it is their will, great healing will take place. If not, then your friend must resign himself to continue his journey as Skinwalker."

Lane nodded her understanding, she had witnessed The

Blessing Way ceremony performed by Jo and understood the significance of the Enemy Way ceremony. She stood back next to Beckett as Jo explained them to Jude.

"My people are known as the Dine☐ or what you know as the Navajo nation. These ceremonies have been handed down to us by the Ancient Ones, the Anasazi. They were given to them by the Holy People and are not used lightly. The Enemy Way ceremony has long been used for warriors returning from war, to cleanse them of the blood and the death, to exorcise the ghosts of those they have killed. Sometimes it is used to banish evil from a soul, such as the evil that has attached itself to your soul in the form of wolf. The ceremony will aid in the banishing of wolf, but you have to be strong. Wolf will fight for its survival and only one of you may come through this."

Beckett was pale and was about to interrupt Jo when Lane's voice in his head restrained him. *Leave it, Beckett. To question him will undermine Jude's confidence in him. He knows what he's doing.*

He remained silent, eyes on Jude's face which was expressionless, giving nothing away and he was reluctant to read him again so soon after the terrors he'd seen unleashed.

Jo's voice was low and steady, hypnotic almost with its Native American inflections as he continued to explain the ceremonies.

"The Enemy Way will drive out evil, but you should remember that Wolf is not by nature an evil creature, taking life only to survive. It is the element of evil men in Skinwalker that makes it evil. Wolf will struggle against this evil just as you will struggle against wolf."

Jude had said nothing and showed no emotion whilst listening to Jo, and then he said, "I will do whatever you tell me I must do, Sir."

Jo's walnut features creased into even more wrinkles as he smiled at Jude, "Jo" he said, "Call me Jo."

"Well, Jo, I will do whatever you say. What about the

other ceremony? Is it how it sounds, a Blessing?"

Jo nodded. "They are chants more than ceremonies, forming part of a larger picture. The Blessing Way chant forms the core of our beliefs and performed after the healing of the Enemy Way chant will bless your soul and prepare it to continue its earthly journey with the protection of the Holy People. Together they restore Hozho or balance to you. That is enough for now. You should rest. I can sense in you a strong cycle of transformation now it has begun. I can't say how long before you transform again. You must have nothing to eat before we begin but you must drink water freely." He looked at Lane, "Spring water is best, as it is free of contamination." Lane nodded.

"There are preparations to make before we can begin, and you should all know that the chants can take many days and nights before they are complete. First we have to construct the Hogan. The chants must be only be sung in the Hogan. On the way here I talked of this to Darius and he made the necessary calls to order what we need. He is very resourceful. He told me the materials will be delivered to your home within the hour."

"What can we do?" asked Beckett.

Jo smiled, "You can build the Hogan. I understand you have great strength and speed. This is good. This will ensure the Hogan is built in good time. But you must heed my directions."

The door opened then and Sabine strode towards Jude.

Jo twinkled at her, "This is the one who prays constantly for your soul," he said to Jude. "It is well with the Holy People that these prayers come from the heart." He turned to her, "And you have a good heart Sabine. Your people have great spiritual courage and it may be that you will need it. You will play a major part in the healing of this man."

Sabine stood in front of Jude. "I saw you in the woods. I wanted to speak to you but you ran."

He nodded. "I remember. I didn't want to hurt you. There was something in your eyes … I don't know."

"My brother was like you. He died and I did nothing to prevent it. I won't make that mistake again. If you will allow it, I want to stay with you through this."

Jude looked grim. "It isn't going to be pretty."

"I know," she said, "I have already seen."

CHAPTER SIXTEEN: THE HOGAN

Outside in the hallway, Jo put his hand on Beckett's arm. "Lane speaks very highly of you, Father."

Beckett was immediately irritated. "It's just Beckett, Jo. Just Beckett."

Jo raised an eyebrow and smiled at him. "Great Spirit is still strong in you. You may have built the wall, but he waits behind it. Maybe this journey with the Holy People will help you take it down, my friend."

Beckett felt cold, "Well, when Great Spirit stands in front of me and tells me why he didn't answer my prayers for my sister when I'd given my life to him, and tells me why he allowed what I am become, then maybe we'll have something to say to each other. Until then, it's just Beckett, Jo."

Beckett turned abruptly and returned to Jude.

"We're going back to the Cedars. So, if you're ready for this we need to get going. Apparently there's something to build." His voice was steady but he knew his words were frosty.

Sabine frowned at him. "We're ready. Just say the word."

Jude nodded at him. "I need to know that if something goes wrong there's some way of … containing me … this *thing* in me."

Beckett tried to make amends for his attitude. "I'm sure that we can handle it. I believe in Jo Timberwolf and Lane, so I believe they can help you. I'll do whatever it takes, that's a promise."

Jude held out a hand to him. "Thanks, Beckett. I trust you, man."

"Jude has agreed for me to go with you, to be part of

95

whatever happens," said Sabine.

"Let's go then. You two can come with me and Jo will go with Lane. Darius will make his own way. I'll be honest with you Jude. I have no idea what will happen, this is all new to me too, but whatever happens, I'll keep my promise to you." He looked at Jude directly and the meaning was understood.

"That is not an option," snapped Sabine, on track with their unspoken agreement.

Beckett shrugged and led the way out of The Sanctuary to his old Jeep and as Sabine tried to climb in beside Jude he put a restraining hand on her arm. "Just humour me; I want you to sit in the front."

"I'm not afraid of him."

"Well maybe you should be", he replied tersely.

The drive to The Cedars was tense and nobody spoke. In contrast to Lane and Jo who were both relaxed and chatting constantly; old friends catching up rather than two people about to embark on a deadly endeavour. As they neared Lane's home the mood became more serious.

"Your friend is troubled," said Jo.

"He's having trouble with what he's become. Mainly because I gave him false hope that it could be cured. Now it looks as though that's not possible."

"No. I think it's something different. His soul has accepted his new form. I believe he has another journey ahead of him."

Lane understood his meaning. "Good luck with that Jo. He shut his God out of his life ten years ago and the wall he built is added to daily brick by brick. It's going to take C4 to pull the bloody thing down."

Jo chuckled and let the subject drop.

As they pulled into the drive of Lane's place, a lorry was already unloading the materials to build the Hogan. Darius had done well. Lane made a mental note to tell him so.

Jo was instantly out of the car and inspecting the

building materials and Lane was pleased to see that he seemed happy with everything. Beckett appeared from the house and strode purposefully towards them. "Is there some sort of plan to follow?" he asked.

"The Diné were taught by The Holy People how to construct the first Hogan for the purpose of the Blessing Way. It has five sides and built around a forked pole and another main straight pole resting on its fork, representing first man and first woman. Once all the secondary poles are in place the whole thing is covered in mud or wood. We don't have time for mud to dry and so my young friend has obtained enough timber to clad the outside. The entrance must face east to catch the first rays of the dawn and those two stone slabs are buried to support the opening to the structure."

Lane and Beckett moved with their vampire speed and strength and in just over an hour, the Hogan stood complete. Jo shook his head.

"Fastest time I've seen a Hogan built. Now I must bless the structure and invite the Holy People to come. The four oak boughs over there will be placed in the four directions to let the Holy People know that a ceremony is about to take place. No rushing that. You can stay if you wish, or you can go prepare the man for what is to come. He needs to take a bath in clear water; no soap and he can drink water. And from now on until the end of the ceremonies no-one but me should touch him."

"I'm on it," said Beckett disappearing into the house.

"I'd like to watch, if that's okay?" said Lane.

Jo nodded his agreement and returned to Lane's car to retrieve his bag fashioned from a Navajo blanket. On his return he tied his old bandana around his forehead and began to chant as he took a bag of white corn meal from his pocket. This he used to anoint the timbers. "White corn meal if the one to be sung over is male," he said, "Yellow corn meal for a female."

Eventually the chanting and prayers were done and Jo

took the rest of the contents of his bag inside the Hogan. Lane watched as he unpacked his rattle and several Hessian bags. He saw Lane's quizzical look. "For the sandpaintings in Blessing Way. Now I must place the oak boughs to tell the Holy People what we are about to do."

"How much does he need to participate, Jo? I mean, what if ...?"

"What if he begins transformation? I was going to talk to you about that. I think maybe if we can keep him subdued it would be advantageous."

"How subdued?"

"I have the necessary herbs with me, though Peyote will not be used on this man, the visions may induce the transformation."

Jo's preparations were lengthy and intense and he finally said, "So shall we begin?"

They walked to the house together in time to meet Beckett in the hallway.

"Where the hell is Darius? He said he was following us. There's no answer from his cell phone or Angel. Where the bloody hell is everyone?"

His feathers were well and truly ruffled and there were heavy creases around his eyes. Beckett was clearly agitated.

"What's up, Handsome?"

"Oh, nothing much. We've got a werewolf in the consulting room, a Hogan in the garden for a ceremony that I have no idea about, and Darius is missing. Nothing's up."

"And?"

"And I'm hungry."

CHAPTER SEVENTEEN: THE ENEMY WAY

Jo had lit a fire in the centre of the Hogan and its sacred smoke drifted from the central hole in the roof structure as he prepared a juniper branch as a sacred staff, adorning it with coloured threads and eagle feathers during which time he had asked for Sabine to pray for Jude's healing.

"It is time," he said. "The Holy People are present and are looking favourably on this man. I must ask you to be his friends and act as his family to witness the healing."

"Does that mean that we can't leave once you've begun?" asked Beckett. Lane knew what he was thinking. He needed to feed and unless he did so within a short timeframe the consequences were unpredictable for him. Jo understood without explanation. He shook his head. "As long as one of you remains, the others may come and go."

"I need to find Angel," he said quietly to Lane. She nodded her understanding. "Be safe, Handsome, and don't be long." She allowed her eyes to linger on his face longer than intended and abruptly turned back to Jo.

Jo began the ancient songs and chanting. Jude had swallowed the herbal medicine willingly and now slept naked on the dirt floor covered with pine branches and flower heads. He tossed fitfully as the chants drew the Holy People to him.

He was aware that he was out of his body and was surrounded by darkness. One by one his ancestors came to him, each with a blessing but not one of them spoke to him. Until a shadowy figure approached him and he was able to 'see' the figure of his grandfather Makani, whose name meant 'the wind'. He looked as he had in life when

Jude had last seen him at his home on the Hawaiian island of Kauai, an older version of Jude himself. He bent over him and placed a Lei around his neck. "For protection Grandson," he said, "And for Blessing. The Goddess Pel protect you and guide you on your journey." He then sprinkled some of the red earth of the island onto his chest. "So you will always find your way home," he said.

Jude was still in darkness but he could see the rough terrain of the White Mountains again, and as if by thought alone he found himself in the entrance to the cave complex in Tora Bora.

The tunnel was in darkness but he could see as though it were daylight. Images flashed by him, images of wolves and men, then men wearing the skins of wolves. They were performing a ritual that had no meaning for him but the darkness that surrounded them made him fearful. One by one the skin wearing men began transforming into wolves. They were down on all fours and the wolf skins now covered their entire body. In the distance the darkness became denser, heavy and almost solid. From out of it rushed a legion of demons and one by one they possessed the bodies of the men. Their fate was sealed and they were doomed to walk the earth as Loup Garoux – the werewolves.

Jude was sweating profusely and Jo bathed his body with tepid water. Lane put an arm around Sabine as she became restless, wanting to go to him but knowing she must not. Jo continued with the sacred songs and Jude's restlessness intensified.

"What's happening to him?" she asked Jo.

"He is with The Holy People. They are showing him the darkness that has attached itself to his soul. Soon he will come face to face with Wolf and they will do battle with the evil. If The Holy Ones will it they will help him to survive."

"And if not?"

"Then we must pray that we can find a more earthly

solution for him. I have not yet found such a solution."

"When will you know?"

Maybe tomorrow around dawn, maybe another day or even two. Only the Holy People know. When he has rested after the Enemy Way he will need to stay strong for Blessing Way which will take three days and nights."

Lane looked concerned and Jo understood her worries. "He will wake from time to time and I will give him water and bathe his body. He will be fine."

She relaxed as Jo began another cycle of chanting over Jude. After half an hour he stopped and took out a woven Navajo shawl from his voluminous blanket bag and gently put it around Sabine's shoulders. "The Ancient Ones have asked me to give this to you."

Sabine drew the shawl around her looking for comfort and finding it. Lane took the opportunity to leave and try and contact Beckett. She dialled his cell phone and it went straight to voice mail and so she dialled the main number at the Sanctuary. It was picked up by one of the volunteers. No, Beckett wasn't there. Neither was Darius nor Angel. Seriously worried she dialled Darius's number and when that went unanswered she tried Angel with the same result. Where in God's name were they? She hoped with everything she had that Beckett had found Angel before the hunger got too much.

A low howl came from the Hogan and she hurried back inside in time to see Jude crouching on all fours with a snarl on his lips. She went for her back pocket ready to pull out her small pistol but Jo raised his hand. "We are in no danger, he doesn't see us. He is with the Wolf spirit and now they will battle the evil one. We must not interfere. Whatever happens now will depend on the strength of his spirit. Wolf is strong in him and he may choose to allow him to do battle alone, but then Wolf will be dominant in him and we may lose him."

Sabine was sobbing quietly and had retreated under the shawl. It was getting dark and although the fire still burned in the Hogan, fed by Jo with branches and logs from the far corner, a chill had settled over them. Jo picked up his rattle and began circling the interior. His eyes were glazed and he looked suddenly ancient.

Lane knew better than to speak to him but tried to read him instead. He was deep in contact with the other world and seemed to trying to drag something away from Jude. In a moment she saw the face of the demon that had attached itself to him, turning him into Skinwalker. There was no light in its eyes, only inky blackness in the void and the intense cold that emanated from it, accompanied by the stench of a charnel house, made her recoil. Jo remained steadfast; a battle of wills between him protected by his Holy People and The Ancient Ones, and the demon protected by a host of nameless evil and the hierarchy of hell. Lane drew in her breath, for once not knowing what to do. The wrong move could finish it for Jude in an instant.

The atmosphere in the Hogan grew heavy and the chill seemed to settle over Jude. Two things happened simultaneously. Jude threw back his head and howled the torment of his soul into the falling night and Jo collapsed onto the floor in front of him.

Lane was on her feet in an instant and Sabine was right behind her. Jo regained consciousness in the next moment and Jude, covered in sweat and flecks of foam at his mouth, fell like a stone.

Jo jumped to his feet, aided by Lane and was leaning over Jude before Sabine had fully comprehended what had occurred.

"He is breathing more easily now. The first part of Enemy Way has removed the evil one from him. Now it is just him and Wolf. He will rest now for many hours, safe with the Holy People. Now we can eat and drink. No alcohol. I will smoke the pipe with The Ancient Ones. Perhaps you should take this opportunity to refresh yourself child," he said to Sabine.

It had been a long day in cramped surroundings and whilst it had little effect on Lane, Sabine was in need of air and a visit to the bathroom.

"I'll be right back," she said hoarsely.

"I'll get some food and drink for you", said Lane. "Shall I bring it here?"

Jo nodded at her but his eyes were closed as he prayed over Jude.

CHAPTER EIGHTEEN: GENETICS

Beckett's phone rang seconds after he had anticipated the call. The screen told him it was Helena Bancroft and as he was about to enter the Sanctuary he simply walked to the other end of the block and swiped his entry card to her lab.

She looked up as he entered and immediately left her work to greet him.

"I just called you," she said. She appeared excited, even though Beckett had realised early that such signs of emotion were rare in her.

"I know. I was right outside. Thought I'd swing by and see you in person. I'm not great on phones. What's up? Last time you called me it was bad news."

"It's not good news. Well, not exactly. I've been approaching this from a different angle. One I'm more familiar with. This vampire thing is genetic as I suspected. Somehow your actual DNA has mutated and is still mutating. I have been trying to 'turn off' the vampire genes, it's called epi-genetics and we refer to it as gene silencing. The research has been done mainly in cancer therapies but it can apply to any disease that is gene based. It's in it's infancy but I think it may be the way to cure the vampirism. But it's gone too far in you, Beckett. I'm so sorry. I really am, but if I try and switch those genes off in you, I'm afraid it could be fatal. The mutation is too severe and now there are more vampire cells than human. It does mean though that if I can manage to isolate the 'mother' gene, the original vampire gene soon after it has entered the DNA then it may work, which means that newly infected or turned vampires should respond to the treatment. We've been working on this for several diseases with varying success for a few years now. I may have a handle on this, although it's early days."

Beckett was silent, assimilating the information.

"Well, I didn't expect a fanfare but you could say something," she said.

"Have you told Lane?" he asked quietly.

Helena shook her head. "Her phone's off. I didn't want to leave her a message. It's too important."

"Do me a favour. Don't tell her yet. She's kinda hooked up at the moment. I'll tell her later and get her to call you. So you think you may have this thing nailed?"

Helena shook her head, "As I said, it's in it's infancy but I believe that it may be the answer. There is a whole lot more to do yet. And it may not work. But I believe it to be the only possible solution."

Beckett nodded his head and ran his fingers through his prematurely grey hair. "Okay, then for the moment, let's keep this possibility between us. Okay?"

"Beckett, it's Lane that brought me here and Lane that pays my salary."

"Actually it's the Vampire High Council that pays your salary and funded this lab. All I'm asking you is until you are sure, let's not raise hopes unduly, eh?"

His eyes penetrated hers and it was she that looked away. "Can I ask you why?"

"Because … because she believes there is a cure for me. If that isn't so then I want to be the one to tell her. Please."

"Some would say that you are fortunate in many ways. You have super strength and speed and your senses are so accentuated that …"

"Stop," interrupted Beckett. "Stop there. I'm sorry if I seem ungrateful for my present state. But the fact is I am having problems with other aspects of it. "

Helena was quiet for a moment and then she said, "You have great spirit, Beckett. You will find a way to be all you are become."

He went pale and stared at her. "What did you say?"

"I said you will find a way to be all you are become."

"I need to go, I'm sorry. Please think about what I have asked you."

"You are my prime patient Beckett, despite whoever pays my salary. But once I know that this is the right way to go, I *will* talk to Lane."

Beckett nodded. "Gotta go," he muttered as he went through the door.

Outside he closed his eyes and took a deep breath. So that was it. He was a vampire for keeps. Well for eternity it would seem. He tried to find some advantages and decided it would keep; after all he had all the time in the world.

The reception area of the Sanctuary was deserted but he detected someone in the adjacent kitchen and from the chemical odour that assailed his nostrils it seemed that instant noodles were on the menu.

He pushed open the kitchen door and startled the young volunteer. He had only seen her there once before but Lane had brought her on board over a year ago.

"Hi, Norma isn't it?"

"Naomi," she replied. "Hi Beckett." She was about twenty he thought and had an intelligent expression. He remembered then, she was a classical music student and music was her life and in her soul and as he reached out to her the music flooded his mind. He smiled at her, more relaxed than he had felt for days.

"Sorry. Naomi. Have you seen Angel? Or Darius?"

"They were here but they both left. Darius seemed in a hurry and after he had gone Angel was worried about him and went after him. Haven't a clue where they went." She poured boiling water into a plastic pot and the chemicals gave off their acrid aroma making him feel nauseous and reminding him of his present hunger.

"When? When did they leave?" he demanded.

"Just after you guys."

Beckett looked at his watch. They'd been gone for

hours.

"They both left you messages though," she said almost as an afterthought. "Behind the desk."

Beckett strode back into the reception area and began rummaging through the various papers on the desk. He recognised Angel's handwriting as his hunger peaked and he felt his incisors beginning their descent. He had to feed and soon whilst he was still in control.

Angel's note was wordy and wandering but the gist of it was that she had left him blood in a collecting bag in Lane's room. She was sorry not to wait for him but she was extremely worried about Darius ... at which point Beckett knew the intensity of the blood lust and tossed the note back onto the desk as he headed for Lane's room, slamming the door behind him.

His eyes were clouded in the now familiar red haze and he snatched at the plastic bag that was inside a thermal pouch that kept it at body temperature scowling at the thought of the anticoagulant in it. But his hunger was above that and he seized it, ripped the seal open and drank. His hunger was rabid and he gave no thought to the savage way he sucked from the bag.

He didn't stop until he had drained the plastic pouch and he felt his heart rate stabilise to its new deathly rhythm then he crossed to the sink and rinsed his mouth and face.

Back in reception feeling a whole lot better he strolled over to Naomi who was deep in concentration on her noodles.

"How can you eat that crap?" he asked, smiling at her.

"I could say the same," she replied in good humour, "but I won't."

"You just did."

She beamed at him. "Better?"

He nodded. "Thanks."

The note from Angel lay where he had tossed it and he read it again slowly this time.

Sorry, Beckett. I just couldn't wait for you. Darius took a phone call from Michael Rabb, I think he said he was the Patriarch, is that right? He was very upset after it and wouldn't tell me about it. I've never seen him in the state he was in. Oh by the way, I left what you need in Lane's room. The battery is dead on my phone so I couldn't call you. I expect you have been trying to get hold of me. Naomi is holding the fort.

He scanned through the note, blah blah blah blah, until he came to the relevant part. The kid really needed a lesson in concise communication.

I waited as long as I could then I went after Darius. I hope I'm in time. Don't be angry with me please, he was in a terrible state. He left you a note too. It's in the envelope on the desk. I'm afraid I read it. I had to know where he's gone.

Beckett shook his head, what the hell was going on?

He ripped open the envelope from Darius without ceremony and went pale. "Oh shit," he said to no one in particular.

"I'll be with Lane at the Cedars if Angel comes back. Get her to call me straight away," he shouted to Naomi as he headed for the door.

She nodded at him and returned to her noodles.

Speed limits went out of the window as he headed down the Brecon road oblivious to speed cameras and he was relieved that all traffic lights were on his side.

Ten minutes later he hurled himself out of his Jeep slamming the door so hard it rebounded and hung open. He was inside in vampire speed and only Lane saw him approach.

She turned her worried face to him as he entered the room.

"Beckett?"

"We need to speak with Mihai," he said. "I don't know what the hell is happening. Darius took a call from him and left in a hurry and in a state. I didn't call him from the Sanctuary; I thought we should speak to him together. Here," he said thrusting Darius's note at her.

She took it and looked up at him, worry creasing her ancient but still beautiful face.

The note was brief and to the point. It simply said, *Gone to Greece.*

CHAPTER NINETEEN: GOING TO GREECE

"What the hell does he think he's playing at? Thinks he's bleeding Shirley Valentine or something!" Beckett fumed.

"Mihai, it's Lane," she said into the phone.

"Ah, Lane, my dear, I called you earlier and spoke with our young friend. I must say he ended the conversation very abruptly. Is he all right?"

"I don't know," she replied tersely, "maybe you can enlighten me. What did you say to him? He's gone flying off to Greece! Quite literally, I presume."

Michael Rabb was quiet for a moment. "That is very unfortunate and very irresponsible of him. I called you but he answered. I asked him to get you to call me back because as I said to you earlier, we do have a problem over there. I told you it wasn't over. The job wasn't finished cleanly, Lane and one of them is still alive. It appears as though the nuns have been caring for him."

"What??" she demanded. "How could that happen?"

"That is what we have to find out. And deal with it."

Lane's face was stone, "Which one? Which one is alive and how?"

"The one that wears the mask."

"Did you tell Darius that?"

Mihai was silent as he replayed his earlier conversation. "I don't think he gave me chance. I may have said it was the younger one. Why?"

"Because I believe he thinks it's his brother Andrei that has survived. And if that is the case, he's gone to finish it. It is all that drove him for years after Andrei slaughtered their parents and when he missed the chance to finish it, he felt empty. This will drive him again until it is over. He won't care that it isn't Andrei; he will transfer his rage and his pain onto Greg Randall just as if Andrei was the one to survive. But he won't be strong enough. Randall will eat him alive."

"When can you leave?"

Lane tossed her chestnut mane. "As soon as I can. Beckett and I are in the middle of something here but we must leave it. I'll make the arrangements."

"No, I'll call our contact at the airport," Mihai replied thoughtfully. "This needs to be done carefully, Lane. We can't afford a mess. Get yourselves to Cardiff as soon as you can and there will be a charter plane waiting for you. I doubt Darius has had that advantage. You may be able to catch up with him if we act quickly. This has to be settled. The consequences of his survival may hasten the inevitable between the Born and the Created. He has to be dealt with. I'll meet you there. Go to Parthavos and take the road to Lourdas about two miles along that road there is the small monastery of Agios Petros. It's where Sister Maria and the other nuns went after the fire. Greg Randall, or Santorini as he prefers to call himself, is with them."

"I understand, Patriarch," she answered formally.

She replaced the receiver slowly and looked over at Beckett.

"I get it," he said to her unspoken words, having both sides of the conversation.

"What about Jude? I'll have to speak with Jo and see if it can still be done with just Sabine and himself. It's a big responsibility for her."

"She's up to it."

Lane entered the Hogan with a tray of food and bottled water for Jo and Sabine.

He lifted his weathered face at her entry and nodded slowly. "There are things in this world that sometimes will not wait. You are torn, my dear friend, but you must go. I will see to this man and with the help of this one with a pure heart we will bring him through." He looked down at

Jude who appeared to be sleeping, though Lane knew better, but here was a hint of peace about his face that Lane had not previously seen.

Sabine still sat huddled in the blanket given to her by Jo earlier in the ceremony. She looked sad and weary as her memories of Abram layered themselves over the present.

"Where are you going?"

Lane put her hand on the girl's cheek, "We have to go. I know you don't understand but we have to." She turned to Jo again. "Is he going to be all right?"

"I truly don't know. The evil is from him but Wolf remains. Only he will be able to defeat him. The struggle is his now. The Holy Ones are watching over him and the Ancient Ones are giving guidance. When he returns from their world, then I will know."

"What about the Blessing Way?"

"Blessing Way will give him peace and strength to continue in whatever form he retains, he will visit with The Holy Ones again and be guided once more by the Ancient Ones. He will make the choice."

"I really have to go, Jo."

"I know."

"Will you wait for me?"

"If the Ancient Ones will it. If not, you know where to find me."

Lane bent and kissed the old man on his leathery cheek. "Thank you Joseph Timberwolf."

"The Holy People go with you, Lane. Wherever it is that you are headed."

Beckett entered the Hogan hand outstretched to Jo. The old man ignored it and stood to embrace him closely. "Remember what I said to you. You carry the light my friend, and sometimes when the light is so bright it blinds you. But the light will always conquer darkness. When darkness is at its deepest the light is still there waiting to shine."

Beckett was about to respond when a low groan from

Jude brought them all to his side.

Jo stooped to bathe his face as Jude opened his eyes. He looked directly at Jo and whispered hoarsely "They said I must go with them. They will need my help."

Jo shook his head. "The Enemy Way should take three days and nights. You are not ready, my friend. Wolf is still strong in you. If we do not complete Enemy Way correctly he may walk with you always."

Jude closed his eyes. "I know. It was my choice. If it wasn't for Lane and Beckett I would have no life. I was ready to end it back at the farm. I owe them."

Beckett interrupted him. "You owe us nothing. Stay here and be healed. Jo has travelled from Arizona to help you get rid of the wolf in you. You owe him that much."

"Everyone is talking of owing," said Jo quietly. "It is not our way. The Holy People have consented to Jude's return for a reason I do not yet know. But they will make it clear to me when the time is right. Blessing Way must be performed and I will ask them for guidance. But if it is to be that he accompanies you then I too will go with you."

"And so will I," said Sabine in a tone that brooked no argument.

Beckett ran his fingers through his hair, "Now hang on a minute. No-one is going with us. What do you think? It's some kind of group vacation? Lane and I have to go and finish a job that we left undone, albeit unknowingly. We have to find one of the most dangerous of our kind and kill him. In such a way as I won't even begin to describe to you. That won't sit well with you, Jo. And you, Jude, you look like shit. You're going nowhere. We can't afford for you to slow us down. And I won't be responsible for any of you. Tell them, Lane."

Before Lane could speak Jude propped himself up on his elbow. "I don't recall asking you to be responsible for me. And I can match you speed for speed and I think you know what I am capable of. I saw my grandfather, Beckett. He told me on behalf of all my ancestors that I have to go with you. He said it was my destiny. Fate has crossed our paths and that is all there is to it. I won't slow you down and you know it."

Lane raised an eyebrow then made a sudden decision. "Then I suggest we get going. Darius already has four hours on us. He'll probably have to fly to Thessaloniki and travel from there to Larissa and on to Parthavos. We will land in Kozani as before and maybe gain back two hours. If we go now."

Sabine looked confused. Jo picked up her hand and said softly, "It seems we are going to Greece."

CHAPTER TWENTY: AGIOS PETROS

Sister Maria knelt in front of the heavily carved altar. Her long black habit draped itself over her heels and her black veil mimicked her once long auburn hair as it fell over her shoulders and down her back. Since the fire at the old monastery of Agios Georgios the remaining nuns of her order had accompanied her to Agios Petros, an abandoned Cistercian monastery whose last remaining monk had died two years previously.

Her prayers ended, she lifted her head to the huge ornate silver crucifix that she had salvaged from the flames at great personal cost. The events of that night lived in her memory as if they had occurred yesterday and she knew they would never leave her until the day she left this world. Inevitably the sight of the crucifix sent her back to that night.

Framed in the glow of the flames that were engulfing the monastery she had raised her hand in farewell and blessing to Lane and Beckett along with their companions Mihai and Darius. She had stood there for a while watching them drive into the distance. Her heart was heavy. Heavy with guilt at what she had been an unwitting party to for many years, deceived by the Mother Superior, Sister Angelique, and the old nun, Sister Agnes. She had believed she was tending the body of their Saint, Agios Georgios when in fact she had been helping to sustain an ancient and most ruthless vampire. And heavy with sadness that her life as she had known it from the age of fifteen had ended.

There were several casualties in the carnage of that night, Sister Angelique being one of them. Maria had evacuated all of the nun's prior to the fire, taking them to the safety of the olive grove on the overlooking hillside. Sister Agnes had passed away naturally the night before and with Maria's new knowledge of the true nature of the convent, she was lost.

Local farmers and residents from the nearby village had seen the flames and wanting to protect their Saint had turned up en masse to put out the flames. She felt her heart would break as she saw their devotion to a lie. But they had quenched the flames in the main part of the monastery and the thickness of the door to the chapel surrounded in stone had done much to prevent it from completely succumbing to the inferno. Beckett had done his job almost too well.

A group of farmers and their sons, it had taken twelve of them, had taken it upon themselves to move the huge ornate silver shrine from the chapel, believing it to be the resting place of their beloved Saint. She knew she could never tell them the truth. Perhaps it was better to leave it to the flames but the villagers would have none of it, transferring it to the monastery of Agios Petros on the back of a dilapidated truck, the usual purpose of which was to transport olives to market. The weight of the shrine threatened to break through the old timbers on the bed of the truck but the owner would have gladly sacrificed his truck bed for the rescue of their beloved Georgios.

As the delayed flames began licking their way across the roof timbers of the chapel Maria had made a last dash inside to drag the silver crucifix from the altar. The crucifix she had lovingly polished to its brilliant shine since just after she had entered the convent years previously.

It was so heavy that she was bent over almost double in the effort, when a falling timber, well alight, crashed onto the altar setting fire to the altar cloth. But saving the crucifix was her only focus. She didn't notice her veil catch fire; her only thought was to save the blessed cross.

Locals had taken it from her as she struggled outside and only then did she feel the searing pain of her burns. In seconds a young man had pulled her to the ground to douse the flames that were licking their way over her habit.

The other nuns had nursed her but the events of that night had left physical as well as mental scars.

Distressed and disorientated they had gone to Agios Petros that night realising that Sister Angelique was missing. Her charred remains had been found the following day clutching an engraving of her only love, Gregori the ancient one.

There had been no formal agreement just an understanding that Agios Petros was to be the new home of Maria and the other nuns.

Maria sighed as she crossed herself and rose from her knees. It would soon be time to ring the bell for Compline. A sound behind her made her shiver. She knew before she turned around who stood behind her.

"Is everything ready for our visitors?" he said in a hoarse voice.

She turned to face him knowing the consequences of alienating this cold and calculating vampire.

"All is ready." *For **your** visitors*, she thought.

Santorini, once the brilliant young haematologist Dr. Greg Randall, had a derisive expression in his face and she knew he was savouring her painful scars. Pain was ambrosia to him. Other people's pain, that was.

"I want you to arrange an opening service to your Saint. I need to feed and my friends will be hungry."

She lowered her head to hide the shame and the tears that came unchecked.

"Please," she whispered. "Please, no."

He ignored her plea. "Of course you must tell them that the body of Georgios will no longer be displayed. Blame the fragility of the remains after the fire. I am finding the silver shrine a fitting place for me."

Sister Maria clutched the end of her wooden rosary. Fitting indeed, since its previous occupant was also a cold, ruthless and savage vampire.

"Your blood is adequate, no more than that. It must be the piety," he said icily. "No matter, it sustains me, but a feast is called for and a feast there will be. Understand?"

She understood too well. There would be those of the surrounding villages and farms that would either return home to waste away and die, or worse, they would not be seen again. Usually young females, it was believed that they had entered the closed order at the monastery. She loathed what she had become but in her distressed state she had begun to believe it a punishment for her previous sin of caring for Gregori. If it was a punishment she would bare it with fortitude.

His eyes were drinking her in and she felt her flesh crawl as he openly appraised her.

"Such a pity the fire marred your looks," he said without emotion, "I may have satisfied other needs if it weren't for the fact that your face disgusts me."

Maria offered a silent prayer thanking God for the scars.

"However, some of our visitors may overlook them."

Blood ran as ice in her veins and she closed her eyes to the thought. Never. That could not be borne.

He read her and laughed harshly. "Are you forgetting something? I know where she lives. Remember that. Mother Superior." His voice was taught and mocking and it felt as though a steel gauntlet was crushing her heart. How many more tests would there be before she was free and forgiven?

"May I go, now?"

He nodded and laughed again, a sound that would always chill her soul. "I know where to find you."

Her habit swished on the flagstones as she hurried from his presence. It was time to ring the bell to call the sisters to Compline and Santorini would return to his rest in the silver shrine as Gregori's self-appointed heir. Only she knew the truth.

Most of the sisters were old, and it had been a

unanimous decision that she should become Sister Angelique's successor as Mother Superior, deciding that her relative youth would bring energy to the position, trading their wisdom and experience for her obvious dedication. They could never know.

She closed the door of her office behind her and leaned against it as if it could keep out all evil. Even though she knew that no door could keep out the evil that lived alongside them. She closed her eyes. *Dear God, help me.*

A gentle knock on the other side made her take a deep breath in an effort to regain her composure. She opened the door and tried to smile at Sister Anna, the new young novice who had been a mere child only weeks before it seemed.

"How can I help you, Sister?" she asked trying again to smile but failing as the still raw burns puckered her cheek painfully. There were no mirrors in their cells and she shunned reflective surfaces, all except the alter crucifix. Vanity was a sin but it wasn't vanity that kept her away from her own reflection, it was shame and raw memory. God had marked her and her sins, now she must atone, but she had no idea how she would ever be able to achieve that. The sin was hers to bear.

"May I toll the bell, Mother? I noticed how it hurt your hands at Matins. I can do it, I have watched you often and I know the tone of the prayer bells by heart and I want to help you."

Despite the pain Maria smiled at the young girl. "You are very kind, Anna. You have a big heart." She was about to refuse gently, but something burned in the young novice's eyes that momentarily shocked her. It was wisdom beyond her years and something else. There was a distant knowing that shone from her eyes and there was a hint of herself at that age. She had learned to speak excellent English under Maria's tutelage and her Latin was following swiftly. She couldn't deny her request. To do so would be a selfish act that she wasn't capable of.

"Would you like me to go with you?"

Anna's delight was obvious. "No, I know what to do. Please stay and rest before prayers." She was gone in a flurry of habit and rosary, humming softly to herself. Anna would not flourish in a silent order.

Maria sat behind her desk and leaned back, allowing herself to relax before leading the nuns in the final devotions of the day. In an unconscious movement her hand strayed to her throat, where the two puncture wounds under her wimple were constantly raw. Santorini had an insatiable blood lust and she had no idea how much longer she could sustain him.

His earlier words tumbled around her mind like heat seeking missiles desperate to connect with their target. '*Are you forgetting something? I know where she lives. Remember that, Mother Superior.*' Only she would understand the derision as he spat the word Mother.

On the night of the fire when the local men had offloaded the silver shrine into the chapel of Agios Petros and she had allowed her burns to be tended, she had returned to the chapel to seek guidance. He had come to her then, clearly weak and with death fast approaching. She had seen Lane plunge the hypodermic into his neck and she had seen him fall and assumed that he was dead. In the chaos that ensued he had obviously found enough strength to remove himself from the coming fire.

She had gasped aloud when she had seen him and the steel in his voice chilled her to her core.

"*Come here,*" he had said. *His voice was weak but his will was iron and he had taken control of her mind. She had no choice but to obey. She felt his eyes probe hers and the insidious tentacles of his own mind writhing and reaching into hers, against which there was no defence.*

After a moment or two he had slumped onto a chair. "I see I have found my salvation. No, not in the cold empty tomb of the carpenter. You are my salvation, my food source. You will nourish me whilst I heal. And I know that you will do my bidding, dear Sister. You see I now know your secret. The child in your womb when you entered the convent. The long and painful birth which you took to be God's punishment. The nun's arranging the adoption. And I see her. Even though you haven't laid eyes on her since her cord was cut, severing her from your belly. I have seen her. And remember this always, Sister Maria. I know where your daughter is.'

CHAPTER TWENTY ONE: THE GATHERING

Compline was over and the nuns had all retired to their cells. All except Maria who had one last duty to perform before bed. Santorini would be waiting for her in the chapel.

Her footsteps were heavy as she approached the huge silver shrine in which he had taken up residence. She knew it was his intention to take over from Gregori in every matter and sleeping in his tomb brought that horrific possibility even closer.

The others like him, intent on a war between the Born and the Created, those who were born vampire and were, in their minds, of pure blood, would be arriving soon and she wanted to be done with Santorini and back in her cell where she would feel removed from the gathering about to take place. The Born agenda was to eradicate all those who had been turned by a vampire, the Created. They had no truck with the enforced Vampire Code and regardless of death and suffering, fed only in the traditional way. Directly from a human vein.

As she neared the shrine, heavily ornate and of ancient silver, the sanctuary light reflected its warm steady glow along the side of the tomb. Maria shivered; it was as if the resident of the tomb was seeking a blessing. Well she would deny him that if nothing else.

For the first time since she had entered the convent, she trod softly to the sanctuary and gently snuffed out the perpetual light. Since a child of fifteen, pregnant and homeless when the nun's had taken her into their lives, she had taken comfort from the sanctuary light in the chapel. It was after all, its purpose.

When her child was born and adopted she had decided to stay with the nuns and soon afterwards she had put on the habit of a novice and it had been her daily task to ensure the sanctuary light never went out. She tended the flame as if its life had been that of her child. And now she had snuffed it out. Santorini would take no comfort from a light of such purity.

A mocking laugh brought her thoughts to the present.

"You are truly pathetic. I need no light. I am a creature of the darkness and glory in it. I have no need of you tonight. My thirst is quenched. You may go."

Sister Maria frowned at his words, not comprehending at first, and then the terrible truth felled her like a kick in her gut. She looked around frantically in the half light of the chapel until her eyes settled on the tip of a shoe protruding from behind the great silver coffin. She sucked in air and held it there as she stepped towards it. And as she moved closer she saw what appeared to be a bundle of black rags. Her mind fought between obliterating the sight and allowing her understanding of what was in fact the body of one of the older nuns, Sister Theresa. She lay in a bloodless heap, no drop had been wasted. She crossed herself and fell to her knees at the side of the old woman.

"Why?"

"Why? Because I was hungry and you were late. And because she returned to the chapel after your futile babble to be alone with her saint. Ha! Well she was alone with me and I showed her the truth."

"Your truth. It has no place here."

She didn't see him move but he was in front of her, his face an inch from hers. She didn't back away.

"You need to be more respectful. Have you forgotten my promise? I will go to her and drain the life from her. But only after I have had my pleasure from her in ways that you could never comprehend. Be careful, Mother Superior", he mocked. "Your usefulness is limited."

Several sets of footsteps sounded in the corridor to the

chapel. Santorini grabbed her and thrust her towards the side door.

"Disappear."

An instruction she would gladly obey. At any other time. She exited through the small side door but as she closed it she left an inch gap. She had to see who had arrived. It was her responsibility now.

The chapel door opened slowly and the dark figures strode towards Santorini, led by a tall slim man with the darkest brown eyes and ebony wavy hair that rested on his shoulders. He favoured the gothic way of dress as had Gregori, and around his mouth the hint of cruelty and amusement that had become familiar over the years. Markos Vasilakis proffered his hand to Santorini and bowed his head in greeting. "So you are the protégée of Gregori. The House of Vasilakis is at your service. He nodded to the other two, "This is Angelos and this is Constantinos, they are my cousins and also of the House of Vasilakis." The others nodded their greeting to him. They were also of obvious Greek origin and although they were dissimilar from Markos in many ways, the same cruel slant around the mouth confirmed them as family.

"It is an honour to receive you, however humble the surroundings."

"Gregori would have been pleased to see you so highly regarded among our kind."

Pleasantries appeared over very quickly and business was soon on the agenda. "I understand you have something for us."

Santorini smiled at him and nodded. "I have. I have enough of the anti virus to take out several hundred, at my home in Wales. And more importantly I have the formula."

"But I understood that you had been killed by this substance. How is it that you survive?"

"Because Gregori's blood runs in my veins now; his blood is now my blood."

"Gregori may have been your sponsor but …" He left the sentence unfinished.

Santorini fumed inside. How dare this man stand before him and try and ridicule him. Well, he would need to sing a different tune if he was to receive a share of the anti HVV. He smiled again, insults were insults but he had the upper hand.

More movement in the courtyard announced further arrivals. The Romanian House of Tepes were keen to possess the anti HVV. There were altogether too many Created in the Carpathians.

Markos Vasilakis strode out to meet them. He embraced the one at the front of the small group. "Vasile. My House does you honour."

"Markos, a pleasure. My House as always is your House. Have you met with him?"

Markos nodded his affirmation. "He appears to have what we need to complete this cleansing. But he is not stupid. He was after all Gregori's hope."

Vasile Tepes, born in Sighisuara, in the heart of the Carpathians in Romania, in the house and birthplace of his great grandfather, Vlad Tepes, known to millions as Vlad Dracul, looked grave.

"He is fortunate that we have need of his work. I would not bear his insolence under other circumstances. But for now we humour him. The Vampire High Council has the number of their days, this pretender to Gregori's throne will see to it. Their so called Vampire Code is an obscenity and will not be tolerated when the Born are in control. Does he know of the heir?"

Markos shook his head. "No, Drakos has instructed that the pleasure be his. Once we have what we need. Come my friend, I will take you to him. You should know that he doesn't have all of the serum with him. He has some I have no doubt, but the bulk of it is in Wales. Once we have the formula however, we will have no need of his stock. "

Inside the chapel, Santorini waited to greet the House of Tepes. He could not read their thoughts; these were indeed ancient ones, able to cloak their minds against even their own kind. Had he been able to do so he may have reconsidered his position; as it was he greeted the newcomers with deference.

"Vasile, welcome. You do me honour to see that the House of Tepes has sent one of its highest nobles to this gathering of the Born."

Vasile exchanged formal greetings with Santorini and introduced his companions as his brothers, Luca and Mircea. Over the following hours, representatives of the other Houses arrived, making twenty in total attending the gathering. Santorini felt slighted but consoled himself with the knowledge that he had what they all wanted and they would have to allow him access to their enclave before he would part with anything.

CHAPTER TWENTY TWO: NOT A LEFT OVER

"I know the anti virus obviously doesn't work," Lane said, exasperated. "Because Santorini is still alive and kicking and stirring up the Born in Eastern Europe. But it incapacitated him enough so we thought he was dead. I tell you Beckett, we can use it against them. It will buy us time if we're up against it."

"I know what you're saying, but it does involve getting up close and personal before we can use it. I still say the silver nitrate and anti HVV bullet is better."

"The anti HVV only works as a weapon on the Created, it will have no effect on the Born. They are bent on a war and if they get whatever this is from Santorini, it will happen. And thousands of innocents will die."

Beckett's face was stormy and she read him, "I don't know why you didn't die, Beckett. Or Santorini."

"I do," Helena Bancroft stood in the open doorway.

Everyone spun around and eyes were fixed on her. She carried a bundle of papers and tossed them onto the table. "It didn't kill you, Beckett because you have an immunity."

Beckett frowned in question.

"Immunity to what?"

"I'm guessing you still have your appendix?"

Beckett nodded, even more puzzled.

Lane was quick to read her, "I see where you're going with this."

"Well perhaps someone would be good enough to enlighten me."

"Sorry, Handsome. Helena?"

"For years we believed that the appendix was nothing more than a left over from the time we ate leaves and the

131

appendix housed certain bacteria which would break down the large amounts of cellulose. We were wrong, at least in part, it's now very apparent that the appendix plays an important role in our immune systems. I have found significant numbers of these bacteria or at least the antigens they produce, in your blood Beckett, but they were neutralised by the anti HVV. If I'm correct it is these antigens that produce antibodies designed to combat the mutagen from the vampire. Those treated with the serum that have parted company with their appendix will die. I don't believe Greg Randall had the full handle on this, although he was half way there. It seems from what's left of his research that his agenda was to kill the Created from the beginning. It was never about saving those just turned at all."

"So it's not genetic? It's viral after all?" Beckett's voice was getting louder.

Helena shook her head, oblivious to the suggestion of the possibility of having been wrong. "Actually, it's both. A mutagen is a physical or chemical agent that has a direct effect on the DNA. The vampire mutagen is passed through human body fluids, just like HIV. In the saliva of the bite mainly and if it gets into the digestive tract, in other words if the vampire blood is swallowed, it's a done deal."

Beckett paled. "Great. You're going to tell me I have AIDS next."

"No, but it *is* Randall's research into AIDS that led him here. His anti HVV is nothing more than a vehicle for turning off the antigens produced from the bacteria in the appendix."

"What about the Born, why doesn't it affect them?"

Because the Born, as you call them, are almost a separate species. Their DNA was mutated so long ago that it replicates perfectly in their offspring. Two vampires producing a child will always produce a pure blood vampire. Their own immune systems effectively eradicate any human DNA. Your silver nitrate bullets won't kill them either, but they may slow them down. I'm afraid it's the old way or no way with them."

"Better load up then," muttered Beckett.

"I haven't quite finished," she said quietly. "There's one thing I need to be sure."

Beckett was pacing up and down, his hands on his hips, his frustration oozing from every pour. "And that is?"

"A sample of Randall's blood."

"Get what you need. You're coming with us," Lane said quietly. She turned to Beckett, "I need to talk to you outside."

He followed her into the corridor where she stood arms folded leaning against the wall, her right knee bent so the sole of her black leather booted foot was against the wall and her face was stony.

"Okay, Handsome, let's do this now before we get too deep into the shit and it affects the outcome."

"What?"

"Exactly. What. What the hell is wrong with you? It's time for the poor Beckett scenario to finish. You are like me now, a vampire, a being who will live to God knows how old. Living off human blood in the most ethical way we can. From people who voluntarily save us from starvation on a daily basis. You could be dead, or worse, Undead. But you're not, you're alive and you should be happy, not going about as if no-one else suffers. Get with the programme Beckett, or …"

In a movement so fast, that even she was caught unawares, Beckett lunged forwards against her, pressing his hands into the wall just above her shoulders. His mouth was on hers and he was kissing her so deeply that her ultra slow breathing speeded up to almost normal.

Shock was her first response but she resisted its follow up to push him away. Seconds later she was returning his kisses, her arms in mid air, wanting to hold him but not daring to.

Eventually he pushed himself off the wall. His face betrayed his shock at his own action and the heat of her response. "Um, I'm sorry Legs. I don't know what came over me. It's just that you looked so damn sexy leaning against the wall like that, and ..."

Lane smoothed her hair and looked away. She had wanted him to do that for such a long time and hadn't realised it until that moment. Now he obviously regretted it. She daren't look at him.

"... And you're right," he said, effectively changing the subject. "I've been an asshole. I don't deserve a friend like you. Any of you."

The word 'friend' hung in the air between them like a wall that both were afraid to scale.

"Yes, well, that's what friends are for. You okay?"

"Yep. You?"

She nodded, "Yep. Let's go, Handsome. I'm afraid for Darius."

The mention of the boy pulled at Beckett. This had to be about Darius first, Santorini and the others later. Though the two were about to be inextricably linked. There was going to be a lot of blood spilled. Old and new, Born and Created.

Helena had already left for her lab to pack only the most necessary of her equipment and Jude, although subdued, was on his feet and ready to leave. Sabine seemed over anxious but insisted that she was fine and ready to go. Jo was distant and contemplative, communing with his Holy People. *Good*, thought Lane, *We're going to need all the help we can get.*

In little less than an hour, Lane and Beckett had packed their guns and the ammo loaded with small explosive charges that would send liquid silver nitrate throughout the body of its victim. Lane had pushed her ancient Toledo steel blade that opened into a sword into her boot and fastened a dual shoulder holster under her leather jacket. In her inside pocket was the large scalpel that would sever the heads of those she killed and then remove the heart. No-one that stood against them and died would be allowed to rise again.

Sabine went paler by the minute watching their preparations. It didn't go unnoticed.

"I don't know why you want in on this," said Jude. "Why don't you stay here? I'll come back, I promise."

"And why do *you* want in on this? It's not your fight."

"Well, I think it is. I'm not so different from them. And I owe them."

"You don't owe them your life."

"I think you're wrong. At least I have a life. I have no idea what is going to happen to me or how I'm going to live with it, but I do know I am what I am for a reason. That much was made very plain to me."

"When?"

"When I was with The Holy People and the Ancient Ones. Nothing was said, I just know."

"I'm coming with you." Her voice was barely above a whisper.

He nodded and reached inside his jacket, "Then you'd better have this. Aim at the head, you may miss the heart." He passed a small pistol to her, his personal small arm whilst he had been in the SAS.

"I never miss," she said. "My family are Rom; we live in and from the countryside. I have never missed a rabbit for the pot nor have I been such a bad shot that the animal suffered. I won't miss the heart."

"It won't kill them, just slow them down and bring them to their knees. Long enough for them to be dealt with."

Images of the blades the other's carried drove the blood from her face again. "I understand."

CHAPTER TWENTY THREE: DARIUS

Darius had been luckier than Lane anticipated. By the time she was reading his note, his flight had landed in Thessaloniki. Thirty minutes later he was heading away from the airport in a hired Jeep. Fast.

In the hour and a half it had taken them to prepare for the journey and what lay at its end, Darius was driving into Parthavos, a mere two kilometres from the monastery of Agios Georgios. It had been easy to get out of Mihai where the nuns were located, and the young survivor.

As the narrow road wound around the hillside speckled with olive and lemon groves the scent of the trees wafted on the night breeze. Two minutes later he rounded the corner of the road to come face to face with the charred remains of the old monastery. It's burned out bell tower pointed heavenward like an accusing finger. Its roof was gone along with its bell and its blackened walls stood like monoliths against the darkening sky.

Darius stopped the Jeep and jumped out. He stood watching, replaying, rewinding, this time it would be him that dealt the final blow to Andrei. It hurt, deep inside as he remembered their youth and how close they had been, playing in the garden of his parents London home. Parents who had fled to Britain a year before Andrei was born, leaving Budapest for the relative safety of the West. Andrei was fifteen years older than Darius and he couldn't remember when his brother had changed, but he remembered the night that Andrei had come home late, and in a rage had slaughtered their father where he stood and ripped open their mother's throat seconds later. Darius had been ten and he had run. He had run fast and far and had spent the rest of his life seeking the courage and satisfaction of revenge. Now it was close. Mihai had said it was the younger vampire that had survived. It could only be Andrei.

He took a deep breath and jumped back behind the wheel of the open Jeep, crashed the gears and took off with the screech of tyres on old concrete.

The moon was low over the monastery of Agios Petros, illuminating the road and any vehicle that approached. He stopped, threw the gears into reverse and backed away. No point in announcing his arrival.

A hundred yards back the road passed through a small copse, he slowed to a crawl and pulled the Jeep off the road into a small stand of trees. Shelter enough for the Jeep. Shelter for him on arrival was another matter. He had to do this right, had to find Andrei unawares. It would be his only advantage. He would take a chance that he was too busy to detect his scent or hear his approach from a distance.

In Larissa he had purchased a hunting knife; a gun would have been possible but would have taken time and in any case he didn't have the silver nitrate ammo. The knife would do its job if given the chance. There would be no running this time.

He thought of Beckett and Lane, more like parents and the only family he had known for many years. He was sorry to have run out on them, but if he had waited they would have taken over the show again, and again he might be frustrated as he watched another's hand end Andrei's life. He was deep in thought and memories and didn't become aware of the other headlights until they were upon him. He jumped into the shelter of the trees and watched as the other vehicle, another hired Jeep pulled up beside his.

He stood behind a tree and watched as a young girl got out of the vehicle slowly. *Angel ?* What the hell?

He processed the information and his options quickly. If he stayed put she may go away. But what if she went on the monastery? She'd be alone with the vampires who had no scruples about taking a life.

He made a decision and ran into the road.

Angel let out a small scream of surprise. She was pale and shaking. He grabbed her by the shoulders.

"What the hell do you think you're doing? How did you get here? How? Tell me!" He was shouting and suddenly realised he had been shaking her. He dropped his hands and lowered his voice.

"Tell me."

"I followed you," she said, half sobbing. "I was on the same flight as you, I was careful that you didn't see me. I knew you'd react like this. I wasn't about to let you go into this on your own, Darius. I'm sorry."

"So am I. Now I have to think about your safety."

"What about yours? You don't seem to care what happens to you. But I do. And so does Beckett, and Lane. I'm here and I'm going with you."

"Oh, no. No you are not. No question. You are going to get back in your car and drive back to Parthavos. Wait for me there."

The glint of defiance was bright in her eyes and he knew that nothing he could say would change it.

"Fuck!" he yelled. He let his head fall and couldn't look at her. After a few moments he said, "You do *exactly* as I tell you and on no account are you going in with me. You can wait outside and if I don't come back out within the hour, you get back to Parthavos and wait there. I have no doubt that Beckett and Lane won't be too far behind. *Understood?*"

She nodded tearfully, her dark eyeliner making black rivulets down her cheek.

"It's on foot from here, just around the corner. And quietly. Don't speak, don't say a word. Their hearing is so acute they can hear a mouse fart in Athens. I'm banking on them being busy or distracted. Enough to let me get in there."

139

He saw the stubborn look he'd come to associate with her. "I *mean* it. You do as I say or I'll knock you out cold here and now and bundle you back in your Jeep. Your choice."

She nodded. "Okay. I'll do as you say. Just promise me you'll come back and wait for Beckett if it looks too dangerous."

He didn't reply.

"Darius! Promise me."

"Yes, all right. Now let's go. Stay behind me and no sound."

CHAPTER TWENTY FOUR: THE RETURN

Beckett refrained from speaking his thoughts about their trip, it had increasingly become like a *charabanc* outing. He made sure he sat next to Jude on the aircraft, much to Sabine's disapproval. He was concerned that despite the man's convictions, he was in no shape for what awaited them. And he didn't want to be in such close proximity to Lane.

Jude listened to him quietly then took hold of Beckett's arm.

"Forget the wolf thing. I'm ex-SAS Beckett. I can handle myself. And yes, I know what they are capable of but I'm up to it. Are you?"

"Of course."

"Then let's go kick some blood sucking arse. No offence."

Beckett was smiling before he realised it. "None taken. I've been thinking. What are you going to do after this?"

Jude shrugged, his piercing eyes not shy of penetrating Beckett's defences. "I'm going back to Afghanistan. There's a whole army of werewolves in those caves, Beckett. I can't leave it. Someone has to take a stand on that. Zero tolerance."

"Need company?"

Jude's surprise was evident. "Well, I didn't expect that. Can I ask why?"

Beckett was quiet for a moment, becoming serious, "Well, let's just say it's only fair. You're here for us, so I'll come with you."

They were in the air rapidly, courtesy of the Vampire High Council's network that extended to the airports and ports and their trip had been put in place by the Patriarch. Mihai had extensive influence. The seat belt sign was off and Lane stood up and leaned over him. A small charge of electricity passed through him, her scent was in his nostrils and rapidly filling him, her energy was everywhere. What had happened, what had changed? Somewhere along the line their relationship had shifted. It was uncomfortable and he sensed regret in her. Damn it.

Landing at the small airstrip of Kozani they were met by Dimitri Petrides, a human who served the Council well. He cleared them through customs rapidly with no inspection, and given the arsenal they carried with them, Beckett sighed with relief.

Lane spent some time with him before returning to the others.

"Mihai is waiting for us and Dimitri will take us to him. He felt that the least waves we make at the airfield the better. He's at the hotel in Parthavos with a car."

They were quiet on the short journey and Beckett knew, like him, Lane was reliving the last time they were there, the time they came to rescue Kat. His thoughts turned to Kat, his patient who had been a Latent vampire and turned by Andrei Marinescu, Darius's older brother. He had thought himself in love with her, and in a way he had been. But they had never been lovers, even before the turning. After it was all over and Kat had died in the monastery he thought his heart would break. It was Lane that saw him through that and it was Lane that had made him realise the truth. His love for Kat was born out of his loss of Grace, his sister who had died at the hands of Santorini when it had all begun. Several lifetimes ago it seemed. He had transferred the love from one to the other and he had felt as responsible for Kat's death as he had for Grace. Beckett had carried the guilt for too long and now he had transferred that guilt onto God. In the words of the poet, he was fucked up.

He looked over at Lane who had her eyes closed, but

he knew that behind the eyelids the scenes were similar to those in his own memories. Memories that now played out as if they were happening right then.

"They're not in the chapel." Lane stopped and sniffed the air. *"There's been a death."*

Beckett paled.

Lane shook her head, "It's not her. The others are together, we have to be quick; they'll already know we're here. Move."

Before they could obey her, Santorini appeared in front of them, his canines were down and ready, he hissed and launched himself at Lane who had no time to fire the gun.

Santorini took her down and raised his hand to strike. His fingertips glowed in the half light. On each fingertip he wore a gold sheath with a lancet in the end and he prepared to put an end to Lane. Darius came from nowhere and threw himself onto Santo's back, clasping him around the neck. The masked vampire roared with rage and flung the boy off like a feather, kicking him with savage intensity in the side of the head. Darius lost consciousness as Beckett was propelling himself into Santorini from the front. The gold lancet tips caught his throat, but didn't bite deep. Beckett felt the warm blood trickle down behind his collar. He turned on Santorini again as Lane caught him from behind.

Before she could act further, Nik and Gregori were on the scene. She turned and fired blindly as Beckett lost his grip on the wooden stake. It clattered to the floor and Santorini took the opportunity to grab Beckett by the throat and hurl him against the wall. His eyes were ruby holes in the silk mask as he gave vent to his true nature and his fury.

Two of Lane's random bullets had found a home and Nik was sliding to the floor with a stunned expression. Gregori roared in wild rage and leaped at Lane. "That's my son and you'll pay for that."

He grabbed at her and twisted her around, pinning her

to him, as he grabbed the blade from her and held it to her own throat.

There was a shrill keening noise that came from Kat as she arrived to see Nik lying on the floor in a widening pool of blood. Mistaking his assailant, she snatched the stake from the floor and rammed it home into Gregori's back.

He arched his back and momentarily relaxed his grip on Lane but it was long enough for her to pull free. He spun around to face Kat and grabbed her by the hair, pulling her to him in an easy gesture. Beckett ploughed towards Gregori who was still dragging Kat by the hair and with the stake protruding from his back as if it was a toothpick.

"Ah, shit," spat Beckett, as Santorini lunged at him, again deflecting his contact with Gregori.

Lane reached inside her jacket but Beckett couldn't see what it was that was in her hand. In less than a second she was flying towards Santorini, her arm raised. She brought it crashing down into the side of his neck then Beckett saw that it was a syringe. She rammed the plunger home and jumped back to watch as beneath the mask his face suffused red as his blood vessels dilated and reacted to his own Anti-HVV. Santorini was dying.

But he hadn't died and here they were again. This time it had to be finished.

He shifted in his seat as Lane lit another cigarette. He smiled at her and she was prepared for the usual reprimand to which she would give her usual reply, amounting to two fingers, but it didn't come.

"I don't suppose you've got one to spare?" he asked.

She laughed aloud, "Okay, but we haven't got time for you to choke and cough up your lungs."

She passed a cigarette to him and proffered the flame on her gold lighter. He inhaled cautiously much to the amusement of the others. Only Helena opened her mouth to protest but thought better of it. She was on a journey to she didn't know where, and second hand smoke featured low on the list of her concerns. And if what she had been told was even a half truth, she didn't know who would be returning, so if a cigarette made him feel better, so be it.

"I could get used to this," he said. "As you always say, it's not going to kill me."

Helena refrained again from commenting on *her* vulnerability.

The small village of Parthavos with its one taverna come hotel nestled in a hollow in the distance and each one of them fell silent.

Dimitri stopped the car outside the tiny hotel. Darkness had fallen but even so there were very few lights to be seen. It was always that way in Parthavos. They had learned a long time ago not to attract unwanted attention. Lane got out of the vehicle first and headed for the front door. There was movement inside and Mihai was in front of them instantly.

He was dressed as always in a black silk suit and black polo neck jumper. His long hair shone in the moonlight like a silver dollar and it was pinned at his neck with a diamond hair ornament that was probably as old as he was. He put his arms around Lane and pulled her to him then kissed her on the top of her head. Beckett felt something fire inside him that was as unfamiliar as it was unpleasant.

Mihai let her go and moved forward, hand outstretched to Beckett.

"Good to see you, Beckett. I'm just sorry we meet in the same circumstances."

Beckett grinned at him. "Not quite Mihai, last time we didn't know which colour coat you were wearing until the last minute. Dodgy ground, one of us might have done for you."

Mihai threw back his head and laughed. "Or perhaps not," he said. His eyes scanned the remainder of their party. "Lane? Perhaps you will explain?"

Lane was quick to respond. "Mihai, this is Dr. Helena Bancroft who we funded to take over research into the anti HVV. She has made the beginnings of a break through. She has come with us because to complete her research she needs a sample of Santorini's blood."

His eyes were dark and penetrating as he reached out into her mind. After a second or two the light returned to his eyes and he was grinning broadly. "It is my pleasure Doctor. I hope that we will be able to gain what you need. I would however be most grateful if you would remain in the relative safety of this hotel. You must tell me if there is anything you need and it will be obtained for you. He picked up her hand and planted a kiss on the back of it.

Smooth bastard's free with his kisses, thought Beckett irritably.

Mihai's eyes came to rest on Jude.

"Jude Mason," said Lane. "I told you we were in the middle of dealing with something, when we first spoke. It seems that Jude is afflicted in a similar way to us."

Mihai interrupted her before she could continue. His nostrils had been continually sniffing and his eyes had darkened again, probing and reading.

"I know what you are, friend. And I see why you are here. Your help is most welcome, but I'm afraid I cannot guarantee your safety."

Jude shook hands with him, "I don't look for guarantees. I hope I can help."

"Special Forces, I see. Well, even in human terms, that has to be of assistance. Your help is most welcome."

He turned to Sabine and spoke to her in a Romany dialect. "You are Rom I see, and from an ancient family. I knew your ancestor Abraham Wood before he took his tribe into Wales. I see your role in this clearly enough. Love is a powerful motivation, is it not?"

Sabine flushed and answered him back in Romany, glad that Jude could not understand. "It may be love, Sir, but I'm afraid it may not be returned."

"Love is always returned if it's pure. Did you not know that? Rest easy, child. There is love aplenty in that soldier's heart. It will surface."

Jo had been watching and listening quietly, his face serene but a tell tale crease on his brow told that he was a long way from home.

Mihai bowed to him. "Shaman, I bid you welcome. Though I fear your Holy People will not want to see you shed blood. I would be grateful if I didn't have that on my conscience. Perhaps you too would oblige me by staying here with Dr Bancroft and this beautiful gypsy."

Sabine sparked defensively. "I go where he goes." There was defiance and stubborn determination in her voice and Mihai merely smiled in response.

"I thank you, Sir. I will not shed blood, even tainted blood. I cannot have that stain on my soul. But I can help in other ways perhaps."

Mihai nodded at him and turned back to the hotel. "Come, I will tell you what I know and Dr Bancroft …"

"Helena," she interrupted.

"Helena and Shaman Jo can make themselves as comfortable as possible. I'm afraid there will be no comfort for the rest of us until this is over."

Helena had moved alongside Beckett and whispered, "Won't we all cause comment arriving mob handed like this. This is nothing more than a village."

Mihai heard her whispers from across the other side of the room. He smiled at her reassuringly.

"The people of this village have learned long ago not to ask questions or pass comment. I have paid the owner handsomely to make himself scarce until I say he can return. There is no-one else here. Just us. It does mean that you will have to fend for yourselves however. But I'm sure that is no challenge to someone on the verge of a breakthrough to save our kind. The hotel is empty so please choose your rooms. I suggest you take the large one at the front on the first floor, Helena. There is a large table in there for your equipment. Now, if you will excuse us, time is passing and I need to speak with Lane and

Beckett."

Dimitri hadn't hung around after he had unloaded the bags and Helena's boxes. He was human and whilst he was part of the Council's network, he knew when to disappear.

Mihai looked solemn. "I fear the situation is grave," he said. "The elders of several Houses are at the monastery and more are close by. Vasile Tepes is there and he above all of them is to be feared."

Beckett frowned, "Tepes? Is that …?"

"Yes," replied Mihai, "He is the great grandson of Vlad, and every bit as savage. Don't let his urbane manner deceive you."

Lane was agitated and Mihai knew that she was anxious to be on their way.

"What about Darius?" Beckett asked. "Have you seen him?"

Mihai shook his head, "No. But I sense his presence. He is not alone I fear."

Lane knew instantly, "Angel."

Beckett rolled his eyes. How many more were to be a party to what was unfolding? It was rapidly getting out of control. "We'd better go. Nothing is going to happen to him. Not while I breathe."

CHAPTER TWENTY FIVE: DARIUS AND ANGEL

Angel had done as she was bid and they approached the monastery in silence. Darius was pissed with her, now he had to look out for her and he couldn't afford to be distracted. He felt in his jacket for the knife he had bought on the way. It felt wanting. He regretted not listening to his instinct to raid Lane's weaponry but knew also that he would have been detained at Customs in no uncertain manner.

The layout of Agios Petros was very similar to that of the old monastery with a perimeter wall and huge wooden gate. It was in dire need of paint and some of the outer wall was crumbling but it stood as high as the one at Agios Georgios had and that meant climbing over it. He needed to find the least visible part and hope that he could scale it.

He trod slowly around the perimeter searching for a blind spot and as he turned the angle of the rear wall he found it. The Gods on Olympus were smiling down on him as there were no windows in the rear elevation, though he was not naïve enough to think that sight was their only means of early detection. Twenty feet along the wall, an old gnarled olive tree offered him a climbing aid.

He turned to Angel, "Stay here. And I bloody well mean it. Stay here and don't move. If you hear all Hell raised, then you get out of here and quick. I need to know that you'll do that. I can't go in there wondering where the hell you are."

"I'm sorry, Darius. I just … I'm sorry."

Darius expression softened. "Just promise you'll stay here. Then when it's all over you can buy the first round in the first taverna we find. And if you get bored out here, pray."

His words brought Beckett into the forefront of his mind. He'd been stupid to come alone, but Beckett had been through enough and this was his fight. Nevertheless he wished he could see his lined face and storm grey eyes. He wished he could see Beckett run his hands through his hair in exasperation but he was glad that he couldn't. Andrei was his responsibility and he would accept it.

He thought back to the time before when they were about to enter the monastery of Agios Georgios. He had grown up that night, a man before his time.

Beckett had been in tremendous physical pain that night, in the middle of the turning, despite the administration of the anti HVV. And he, Darius, had been childish and naïve thinking he could offer himself up as some sort of sacrificial lamb. There had been carnage that night and a river of blood had been spilled. He was prepared for what lay over the wall, but realised that if he was caught before he could find Andrei, he was alone. Memories of the protection Lane offered came flooding back.

Lane had been confronted by Sister Angelique, whose only agenda was to protect her love, Gregori. She had leaped forwards and knocked the nun out cold. Then stepped over her inert body and moved forwards. She had pulled a small revolver from her hip. It had a pearl handle and was unmistakably ancient.

"*You can shoot them?*" he'd asked in amazement.

"*They're flesh and blood, or most of them are. They won't die with ordinary bullets; that's why mine aren't ordinary.*"

He'd laughed then, "Don't tell me, they're silver bullets, I thought that was Hollywood."

"*Close, although pure silver bullets are most effective on werewolves I understand. These bullets carry a small charge and they explode on impact, carrying the Anti-HVV and silver nitrate inside the body. Same principal as a tranquilizer gun, it will bring them*" *down long enough for this. From her other boot she had drawn the hilt of what appeared to be another dagger, but when she pressed the ornate hilt, a blade shot out, the length of her lower leg, effectively turning it into a sword. That sword would not be there to protect him this time.*

Angel was looking distressed and he took time to put his arm around her. "I forgive you for following me, and I'm sorry I yelled at you. I just don't want to see you hurt. You'll be fine if you stay here. The circus is going to be in there. I'll be back for that drink." He kissed her on the cheek, a friend's kiss without passion.

The olive tree creaked and groaned as its gnarled old branches took his weight, even though Darius was slight. He pulled himself up to the level of the wall and easily straddled the top if it. He waited for a few seconds to see if there was any sound of alarm from inside. There was none and so in one of his heartbeats he dropped to the ground on the other side.

Unfamiliar with the place he relied on memory of the other monastery to possibly give him direction. He could hear voices inside; several people were speaking at the same time and in different languages and dialects. Although his family was from Budapest he had been born in London but had learned his mother tongue and other Eastern European languages at an early age, and now he recognized the language of one of the voices as Romanian. It was a smooth voice with a cultured accent hinting at nobility from the Carpathians. But not one of the voices was Andrei's.

He realized he had been holding his breath since he climbed the olive tree and exhaled deeply. He swallowed hard and crept towards the rear wall of the building. Again he was holding his breath and his heartbeat had picked up apace.

The wall was warm against him as he pressed himself to it. Turning the corner he faced a row of small windows, no lights burned in them. The nun's rooms. Next to them was a larger window with a small chimney adjacent. The kitchen. None of the windows were open, so no access that way. He knew he would have to go around to the front to get inside and that was the easiest way to be seen. He had no choice.

Hugging the wall he rounded the corner to the front. Again Greece's Gods of Olympus were on his side. The front door stood ajar, he wouldn't have to turn the huge iron ring that would open it and probably make noise. So far so good.

The voices seemed closer now he was at the front of the monastery and still he couldn't identify Andrei. Where was he? He tried to get an idea of the location of the voices and decided they were coming from the right of the door, and judging from the window it was the chapel. The problem was that he didn't know if the door to the chapel stood open, he believed it did as the voices were very clear.

He stood weighing up his options. He could pass the front entrance and risk being seen as he looked at the other side of the building for an open window, or her could slip inside and hope to find somewhere to hole up until he could look for Andrei. He felt the blade inside his jacket, he would not falter and he would not miss.

He made a sudden decision to go in through the open front door. There was a darkened window to the left of the front entrance, possible the office of the Mother Superior. He hoped it wouldn't be locked.

As he centred himself ready for the move, he felt an icy chill from behind, the frozen tentacles of the cold atmosphere coiled and writhed around him, cramping his bowel and filling him with nausea. The hand that grabbed his shoulder felt like a huge claw and then there was an arm around his throat cutting off breath.

The voice was cold as the grave as it hissed, "So, who do we have here?"

CHAPTER TWENTY SIX: LOST REVENGE

Mircea Tepes had one of those faces, once seen never forgotten. Harsh features and cruel lines around the mouth and black holes of eyes under dark caterpillar eyebrows did not make for good looking.

Darius felt rather than heard his sharp canine teeth descend ready for action and tried to pull away but Mircea had him in a vice like grip. In a millisecond he had released him from around the throat and had yanked his arm behind his back and pulled it upwards to the shoulder before the boy could process the movement. Then his knee connected with Darius's spine and he was pounded into the wall creating a long gash down the side of his left cheek. He felt the warm blood running down his face and neck and heard the intake of breath and a hiss from behind him as his assailant detected the scent of the crimson rivulet.

Darius was no match physically for Mircea but he was going to give it his best shot. Even as the thoughts were formulating he drowned in the icy chill and he felt the cold wetness of Mircea's tongue on his neck and face, licking and savouring the still oozing blood, sending shivers shooting throughout his entire body that did not stop until they reached his soul. Darius was in deep shit.

The voice was sibilant and reedy. "Ssuch a pity to wasste ssuch rich blood."

He yanked harder on Darius's arm sending unbearable pain into his shoulder and neck until he was near to fainting.

"I have a mind to ssatissfy my hunger right here, but you will make a very acceptable gift from the Housse of

153

Tepes to the heir when he arrivess. Ssuch a beautiful face, ssuch exquissite bone sstructure," he hissed. And in that moment Darius realised that whoever held him captive was not only of the Born and probably an ancient one at that, but he was also one of the Undead.

He tried desperately to turn and at least see who was about to make him their supper, but only achieved a tighter grip from behind and a knee in the back propelling him forwards through the open door into the dimly lit hallway.

Mircea called out in his own language and the adjacent voices fell silent. There was a sound almost like the soft rush of air when a door is opened too quickly as the other vampires settled like mist in front of them.

The one with the long hair and gothic attire glided forwards and hooked a sharp fingernail under Darius's chin.

"Who are you?"

Darius remained silent.

"Cat got your tongue? Or was it Mircea? Hm?"

Darius was scanning the faces of the others, searching for Andrei.

"Speak!" spat Vasile.

Darius shouted back, "Where is Andrei?"

Vasile Tepes frowned, "Andrei? Marinescu?"

Darius nodded painfully.

A voice of steel from inside the chapel answered him. "I killed him."

He recognised the voice and an avalanche of icy understanding engulfed him. He'd been wrong. The young one that had survived was Santorini and not Andrei. He was still to be denied.

Tears of frustration and anger born of years of hatred spilled down his cheeks, their salt causing the wound on his face to sting. But it was buried by the other pain, the pain of his lost revenge.

Santorini was in front of him then, sneering contempt.

"Well, well, the younger Marinescu. Looking for big brother? Sorry. Too late."

Mircea tightened his grip and following Santorini's gestures, followed him, shoving Darius to the rear of the corridor into a room opposite the nuns' accommodation. Darius was thrown unceremoniously onto the hard bed, winded. Before he could gain his breath Santorini dismissed Mircea and closed the door. The speed of his movements made it seem as though he had materialised right in front of him.

The first blow was to Darius' face, opening up the earlier wound, the second was again to the face, splitting his lip. Blood from the two mingled on his chin but he did nothing to stem the flow because the third blow was to the side of his head sending him to oblivion.

Santorini spat onto the floor. "How beautiful are you now?"

Back in the chapel Vasile Tepes was concerned. "Why is he keeping the boy? Are we sure he doesn't know of the heir? And what of The Ancient One? Is he aware of how precarious is his position?"

Markos Vasilakis shook his head. "His defences against us are weaker than he thinks. I have read him and he has no knowledge of either. He is neither of the Born nor of ancient lineage, he presumes too much."

Vasile nodded. "Good. Then we must keep it that way until Drakos arrives. "

"Drakos, my father, is ready to take over from Gregori but needs The Ancient One to concur," Markos replied.

Santorini returned to the group, his arrogance not diminished after cutting up rough with Darius and although he sensed some tension from the others he couldn't read them.

"Why do you keep him, when he would provide nourishment for us now?" asked Vasile.

"Because even though he truly believes he is here alone, except for the puny human woman outside the wall,

I anticipate a large thorn in my side will not be far behind."

Vasile raised an arched eyebrow.

"Lane Dearing. She has been a source of annoyance to me for a very long time now and when she shows up with the priest I can finally put an end to the annoyance."

Vasile looked thoughtful. "Leonora. I know of her. She is high on the Council, I believe. Perhaps we shall have some sport here. Who is the priest you speak of?"

Santorini sneered. "A pathetic man who once was a priest and now he is nothing. She has taken him as a friend. It will be her downfall."

He put his hand on Santorini's shoulder. "You have done well. The feast is arranged?"

Santorini nodded. "The Mother Superior has sent word to the villages, tomorrow there will be food enough for all."

Vasile continued, "You see yourself as Gregori's successor, I know you were his protégée and he was highly pleased with you. His death was unfortunate and if you are correct, the cause of that tragedy may soon be here for us to avenge him. What about their so called Patriarch? The term in itself is an offence."

"Michael Rabb has other fish to fry. He won't be a problem."

"Then tonight we will relax and drink wine from the local vineyards and anticipate what we shall be drinking on the morrow. You have done well, Santorini. Mircea, would you please go and bring in the girl. We must show her our hospitality."

Santorini bristled at Vasile's presumption that the hospitality was his to give but said nothing. He had the formula in his head and without the respect that was his due, these nobles of the ancients and the Born would be disappointed.

Mircea's expression relayed his enjoyment at being given the task of apprehending the young girl as he moved in the blink of an eye to the outer wall.

CHAPTER TWENTY SEVEN: SIGNIFICANT RISK

Helena Bancroft had a lot to understand. She replayed the conversation she'd had with Lane during the journey.

"Just how many vampires are out there?" she'd asked. *Her voice had been level but Lane could read the apprehension within.*

"There has never been a census, but there are many thousands. Some are the Undead, some are the Born and others are Created or Latents."

"Undead? You mean like Dracula? You serious? I thought we were dealing with mutagens caused by infection but that sounds like something a whole lot different." *Her eyes had bored into Lane's. Lane wasn't fazed.*

"Mr Stoker has a lot to answer for but essentially he is correct. Many centuries ago the original vampire passed on the mutant genes creating our kind. Some of them were killed and their bodies animated by something unspeakable."

"So forgive my constant reference to Bram Stoker, but it really is my only point of reference, are they killed à la *Van Helsing?"*

Lane had smiled at her; the brilliant open mind was already processing information that would send most to the asylum or into permanent disbelief.

"If you mean do we cut off their heads and remove their hearts then yes. It is the only way to deal with the Undead."

"And the others?"

Lane had hesitated before saying, "Sometimes we deem it wise to take precautions."

Helena had understood the implied meaning. "Okay. Good to know."

"There is something else that you should know."

"There is?"

Lane had glanced significantly at Jude. "There is

157

another condition that may be similar; certainly to do with altered DNA."

"And I should know this because?"

Lane had lowered her voice, "Because we want you to try and find a cure."

"A cure for what exactly?"

"For Lycanthropy, for a werewolf."

Her life had become very complicated in a few short days but she was above all a scientist searching for answers. And answers she would find. However surprising the questions. And by the time the others were halfway to the monastery she had her eye glued to the microscope lens. She made a sudden decision and grabbed her bag, sending her chair tumbling backwards. Medical breakthroughs often came after significant risks and this was a risk she believed would take her a long way towards an answer.

Jo had remained downstairs deep in meditation and when she burst into the small room he didn't react.

"Jo!" she shouted.

A flicker of acknowledgement drifted over the old leathery face and very slowly he returned his consciousness to the here and now.

"Jo, I can't just sit here and do nothing. I believe I may have found an answer, well at least the beginnings of one. But if what Lane has told me is right, we shouldn't just sit here and allow them to die. Not while there's a chance. I wanted Santorini's blood to be sure but in the meantime our friends may be in dire need of some help."

He was silent for several minutes, half in this world and half in the world of his ancestors. Eventually he spoke slowly, "The Holy People have told me what you ask. It is well with them, they will guide your hand, and so it is well with me. Where do you want to do this?"

Helena shook her head as if to dislodge an annoying insect, totally thrown by his reply.

"How do you know? No. Don't tell me, my belief

boundaries have been stretched far enough, any more and they'll come twanging back and hit me in the face. Okay, so you agree for me to do this? It is a dangerous thing to do in these surroundings, but I'll do everything I can to prevent any infection. Are you sure?"

"Are you?"

"Ninety nine point nine percent."

His face broke into a reassuringly creased smile. "Then I shall be one hundred percent sure for both of us."

"I would do this to myself, but I had my appendix removed when I was ten."

"Then we should do it now."

Helena looked around her, "The kitchen," she said.

In the kitchen she made a grab at the handle of a cupboard, then another and then another until finding the one that housed the meagre cleaning materials. The labels were in Greek but she made a qualified guess at a serious disinfectant and threw it liberally over the table. Her sleeves were rolled up and she hunted around for a scrubbing brush, turning up her nose at the relic she found under the sink, she grabbed at a roll of paper towel and began scrubbing the disinfectant into the table as best she could. There was going to be no incision but she wasn't taking any chances.

Jo got onto the table and laid flat, his usual serenity coming from him in waves as he pushed the top of his jeans over his pelvis. Sudden doubt flickered across her face.

"It's a long time since my surgical rotation. And this is going to hurt."

"No," he said quietly, "it isn't."

His breathing became slow and deep and he began a low chanting in his Navajo tongue, removing him from his surroundings and removing him from any pain.

She took a syringe from her bag along with a sealed long hypodermic needle which she used in her lab work and some antiseptic swabs. It wasn't ideal not even suitable, but it was all she had.

She took a deep breath and pulled on a pair of latex gloves. She was concentrating hard as she gently prodded his lower abdomen, looking for a point over the right side of the abdomen, one-third of the distance from his pelvic bone to his navel, which would give her the best guide to the location of his appendix.

She ripped open a swab and gently wiped over the area, rechecking the location. Then without hesitation she directed the needle into Jo's flesh, through two layers of muscle, into the cavity at the centre of the appendix and withdrew fluid into the syringe. Deftly removing the needle, she swabbed his skin again and handed him a plaster to cover the tiny puncture that may still allow bacteria from the less than hygenic kitchen to enter him. The appendix was often hidden beneath a layer of bowel and she prayed that her needle had found its true objective and not punctured the wall of his intestine.

Jo waved her away as she started to fuss over him.

"Go and find your answer," he said. "And then we will go and find them." He hoped they would not be too late.

At her make-shift lab that she knew was disastrously inadequate she added some stain to the sample on her slide before putting it under her microscope. After maximum magnification she saw them. The specific antigens that had originated in Jo's appendix. She added a drop of blood with Beckett's vampire virus and watched in horror as the vampire cells killed off the antigens. Too late for him, his vampire cells were too many and too strong as she had feared, but in her heart she knew that someone newly infected or newly turned would present a different picture. The antigens would triumph over a few vampire cells before they could proliferate. And Beckett wasn't alone. If anything happened to any of them because she wasn't there it would be unthinkable.

She injected the contents of the syringe into a rubber capped vial and put it in her pocket, along with a handful of needles and a syringe.

Downstairs Jo was nowhere to be seen, already in search of transport, and a few moments later a loud rattle accompanied by the roar of a fractured exhaust told her he had been relatively successful.

Relatively successful wasn't even close. Jo sat at the wheel of an old pick up truck that would be unwelcome at any scrapyard, but apparently was still used daily by one of the local farmers. Helena ignored the overpowering odour of goat and climbed into the cab beside Jo.

"Okay," she said, "let's go find the monastery."

CHAPTER TWENTY EIGHT: WOLF

Jude was uneasy, something was wrong. A powerful odour assailed his nostrils. He sniffed, turning his head, seeking the direction of the smell. Sabine was instantly alert.

She put her hand on his arm. "Jude?"

He didn't answer, focussed on whatever was outside.

Lane spun around connecting with his eyes. Eyes that were normally a deep indigo were slowly changing colour to luminescent amber. Long course hair had appeared on his face and muscle groups in and around his mouth appeared to be in motion over too many savage teeth. And within seconds his nose and mouth took on the appearance of a muzzle, but with no change in bone structure.

"Stop!" she yelled.

Mihai slammed on the brakes and spun around as Beckett lunged towards Jude.

"Mother of God," he whispered. Then to Sabine, "Get out of the car."

She shook her head, clutching Jude's hand, even as hair appeared on the back of his hands and his fingernails were growing visibly into what could only be described as claws.

Mihai and Lane both had guns in their hands before Sabine even saw them move. When her optic nerves had caught up with their movements, she lunged forwards.

"No!"

Becket held on to her with an iron grip. "Shut up and keep still."

Jude had the door open and was clutching at his clothing. An intense heat was torching through him, searing his guts and causing him to rip away his shirt in a desperate attempt to cool his body. He threw back his dreadlocked head and howled into the night.

He dropped his shoulders and loped to the side of the road, head back, sniffing.

Sabine kicked out at Beckett, and the shock of her boot connecting with the softest part of his anatomy made him let go. She flew after Jude, distressed but unafraid. Mihai's expression mirrored Lane's alarm. They flew forwards silently with Beckett only just behind. What the hell had caused this transformation? A transformation that tradition had it was linked to the full moon. And the moon wouldn't be full for nearly another three weeks.

Beckett's eyes penetrated the dark as if it had been noon and soon saw the answer. The hillside adjacent to the side of the road was littered with sheep. Not all of them alive. Two amber lights low to the ground gave away the position of the marauding wolf that had wreaked the havoc. Blood was all over its muzzle and it stood with ears erect and teeth bared. Snarling.

Jude leaped towards the wolf, and they met in mid air. For a surreal moment it seemed as though they would remain airborne then the two suddenly fell to the ground and there was a frantic bundling of fur, hair and limbs.

Frightened bleating from the sheep left alive was instantly drowned by the sounds of deep growls and savage violence. Two alpha males were fighting it out.

Lane and Mihai stood side by side, guns aimed at the roiling mass of beast and man. The scent of blood drifted on the warm night air, filling them both with a raw hunger. They remained focussed on the tangle of destruction but neither could get a clean shot at the wolf. As the fight continued and then stepped up a notch a series of loud yelps gave notice of one in supremacy.

As suddenly as it had begun the two bodies rolled away from each other and lay suddenly still and silent.

"No! Wait!" Lane yelled at Sabine who had made a dive towards the unmoving Jude. She was ignored and Beckett's grab at her just left him holding her jacket.

Sabine knelt beside him and stared in horror at the huge amount of blood that was slicked over his muscular chest. He was bleeding from several deep gouges high on his face and there was blood over his mouth and chin. Unconsciously her hand had flown over her mouth as memories of Abram in the same condition flooded her. She bent over him wiping the blood from his chest then turned to Lane, "He's okay. It's not his blood."

As she uttered the last word, in a flurry of teeth and red stained fur, the wolf was on its feet and airborne. A loud crack from Mihai's gun, one second ahead of the same from Lane, felled the wolf for the last time.

Jude was on his feet as the wolf hit the ground. He wiped the back of his hand across his mouth. The amber light in his eyes was already darkening and in less than a minute the deep indigo had returned. The hair on his cheeks remained but all eyes were witnessing the dark claws retracting into now hairless fingers.

"He was in kill mode and he had the scent of human flesh. He would have killed again, probably a child."

Beckett put his hand on Jude's arm. "How did you know?"

"I just know. I know how they act and think; I know them now. And the wolf in me took over. Jo said we would walk together; it seems he was right, except in certain circumstances it appears as though the wolf is the stronger. I don't know why it happened when the moon isn't full."

Lane answered him. "I think it could be adrenaline, released in anger or fear or as a defence mechanism. Interesting."

Sabine butted in, "*Interesting?* None of you has asked him if he's all right! Interesting? He isn't a lab specimen!"

Jude grinned at her and the indigo eyes pierced hers. "It's okay," he said, "but thanks."

Beckett looked at him with deep concern; he understood how it felt to become something other than who he had been. He understood the confusion, the denial and the anger. He was still working on the acceptance. His understanding was obvious in his expression and Jude nodded at him and in that moment there was a bond forged that would not be broken.

Lane absorbed the fleeting emotion, "Okay Handsome, time to get moving. He's fine. And from what we just saw, I'm glad he's on our side." She held on to his arm and he felt the now familiar charge of electricity, felt it lodge in the centre of his heart. He stared into her eyes, trying to get past her barriers, but sensed that to do so would be his undoing. Instead he cleared his throat and nodded his agreement.

Mihai was back in the car with the engine started before Jude and Sabine even reached it. As Lane and Beckett climbed inside he said, "You should know that I sense some ancient bloodlines."

The monastery was a mile ahead but Mihai and Lane's senses, so finely developed over the centuries could reach out and scan a location for others of their kind, reading the energy signatures of vampire and human alike. Lane threw out her senses to Agios Petros and looked at Beckett.

"Santorini is there. And so are some of the old ones. I can almost taste the House of Tepes and the Vasilakis clan is there too. Powerful opponents, Handsome. You ready?"

Beckett nodded.

"What about Darius?"

"He's there and so is Angel. I have to tell you, their energy is contained and they are both very still. We need to work on the assumption he's been caught. That means I don't know how much time we have."

"They have been waiting," said Mihai. "Waiting for another. I believe it to be Drakos. If my information on the Born is correct, Drakos is Gregori's heir, he is his oldest surviving son. And when I say oldest, I mean centuries oldest. Drakos was born in Athens in fifteen hundred and ten. He is also Undead."

"Great," said Beckett, "Over privileged *and* immortal."

Mihai remained serious, "The Undead are not immortal, as you know. They just take more killing. I need to speak to you on a serious matter, Beckett."

Beckett second guessed him, "I can't prayer for their souls. Apart from the fact that I'm not exactly a fan at the moment, they deserve to rot in Hell."

Mihai was quiet then he said solemnly, "And what of you Beckett? Or Lane? What of me? Do we too deserve to rot in Hell? Evil is created and born into this world but it can't live when there is love in the heart but it can be healed as the soul leaves the body. You pray for a departing soul and the evil is neutralised. You can leave the judgement to the one who is entitled to judge."

"Is that a lecture? It sounds familiar. I used to believe that."

"You still do, you're just a stubborn priest with too much pride."

Beckett was shocked at Mihai's verbal attack. "Pride? I don't think so."

"Of course it's pride to believe that you know the plan for you better than its architect. Have you for one minute stopped to consider what a difference you can make in this world, given your abilities and your understanding? Is it not pride to ignore what could be considered a gift and not suffering?"

"I don't care about me, but why Grace?"

"Perhaps it took the loss of someone so dear to spark the sequence of events that have brought you here. Especially here. You think of him as a son, I sense. Then be a father and teach your son the value of redemption. His and yours."

CHAPTER TWENTY NINE: THE HEIR

Days earlier, Drakos had left his villa in Athens forsaking his view of the Parthenon and had travelled to south eastern Iraq. Two hundred miles south of Baghdad, between the Tigris and Euphrates rivers, the ancient civilisation of Sumer had flourished four thousand years ago. This had been the home of The Ancient One and so it remained. Drakos knew that to inherit Gregori's territory he would need the sanction of The Ancient One. But the oldest vampire alive spent long centuries in vampire sleep only waking in times of crisis, communicating only through telepathy to Lamia, the youngest female of the bloodline, whose sole purpose was to care for the sleeping vampire.

Few vampires knew that The Ancient One still lived, believing that Gregori had been the oldest vampire. But Drakos knew, and so did Vasile, for it had been The Ancient One that had brought about the death of his great grandfather, Vlad Tepes. The Ancient One was high in their consciousness.

It had been twelve centuries since The Ancient One had awoken to reveal the prophecy that had long since slipped into vampire mythology. The prophecy that foretold the end of all the great vampire houses.

The cave entrance was well concealed and without vampire sight that is all it was; a cave. But to the vampire, what lay behind the cave entrance was their sacred, almost holy ground. Almost.

Drakos trembled as he approached the entrance; he sought an audience with The Ancient One through Lamia. Without that sanction he could not assume Gregori's position. He knew it was going to be difficult; although he

169

was Gregori's son he had been born in Dacia, in the heart of the Carpathians and his alliance with the House of Tepes could cause a problem. It was this alliance that Vasile Tepes sought to strengthen. The two houses joined as one would make a formidable empire. But first Drakos needed the all important agreement.

As he entered the cave an opening appeared in the rear wall, triggered by the genetic signature of the vampire. Once through it, corridors and rooms led off in several directions. Everything was dimly lit and Lamia was nowhere to be seen.

He waited, unsure, a condition with which he was unfamiliar. After hesitating for several moments he began to walk slowly along the half light of the corridor. No sound reached him, everywhere was eerily silent. Even his footsteps caused no sound from his leather soled shoes. His dark hair and beard were neatly trimmed perfectly framing the blackest eyes. At home with the elite of Athens, Drakos was out of his comfort zone.

As he neared the middle of the corridor a movement of air from behind made him halt.

"Who seeks the Ancient One?"

Lamia's voice cut through the atmosphere like steel.

He turned to her, drinking in her cold beauty. Waist length hair reflecting blue black hues draped her upper body, and a skirt of dark silk reached her bare feet, caressing the floor as she glided towards him, staring at him with sightless eyes.

"Drakos of Athens. I seek the sanction of The Ancient One to inherit my father's territory."

"Wait here Drakos of Athens; I will seek such sanction for you."

She left him standing in the corridor as she glided past him to a door at the end. He didn't see her enter; she simply melted from his sight.

The room was barely lit and the massive carved marble platform upon which The Ancient One lay was all that it contained. Lamia approached, head bowed, preparing to link her consciousness with the oldest vampire. She knelt at the side of the platform and raised her head.

It had been twelve centuries since The Ancient One had awoken but now the eyes were open.

The voice was barely a sigh, "Help me to rise, child. Bring him to me."

Outside in the corridor Drakos felt the shift. The air became rarefied and ice cold, even to him. Something was different.

Moments later Lamia reappeared, her demeanour unchanged.

"Come with me," was all she said.

He followed her as she glided into the chamber containing the marble platform that now stood empty. Across the room another door stood open. Lamia passed through into the room beyond without a word. He followed her.

The room was again lit only by the light of one flame that cast dancing shadows in every direction. In the darkest corner, buried in deep shadow, stood a huge seat carved from a single piece of marble on which sat The Ancient One, cloaked even against the vampire sight. The silhouette was motionless.

The sigh wafted to him on the meagre air. "Hhhhhhhhhh Drakos of Athens, you have the sanction you seek. Take the territory of your father, Gregori. But take this also with you. The prophecy is upon the Great Houses."

Drakos didn't move, straining his vampire sight to see through the shadows.

"The prophecy?"

A sigh like the rustling of leaves on the autumn wind filled the room.

"A warrior who is neither beast nor man has allied with those who would seek to destroy us. Our own kind has turned against us in defence of those not of pure blood.

They must be eliminated. It was written in ancient times that when the man beast fought alongside the Created, the great Houses would be doomed."

Emboldened by The Ancient One's attention, Drakos pushed the boundary.

"But I thought that was a myth, perpetuated by our ancestors."

The sigh became an audible hiss and the sudden sound of wings in flight accompanied the movement now in front of Drakos.

The silhouette was changing, growing, rising. And then in front of him, open to his vision, stood The Ancient One.

Ancient hair coiled onto an ancient head, clouded eyes near sightless, were wide open. Shrunken, pendulous breasts hung low on a skeletal frame, and the wings were unfurled though not completely open. Drakos' eyes moved downwards to where the feet should have been and saw instead the talons of an eagle.

Lilitu stood before him in all her terrifying aspect.

Lilitu, the illegitimate daughter of Sargon who had once ruled all of Sumer and Akkadia, was terrible to behold and had been feared as a demon throughout all Mesopotamia. Part demon, part vampire, she was known as The Storm Bringer.

Drakos felt his insides turn to ice under her gaze and dreaded the utterance of another word. He trembled as he bowed his head whilst the rustle of folding wings announced Lilitu's return to the marble seat.

He uttered a startled cry and jumped at the sudden and unexpected touch of Lamia. She didn't speak but turned him towards the door. He knew when it was time to leave.

Now he was on his way to the gathering of the Great Houses to take his place as Gregori's heir. His confidence and arrogance returned once he had left the borders of Iraq. The House of Vasilakis would answer to him. But he had no intention of secluding himself in the rural coffin

172

that had satisfied Gregori. Drakos would reside where he belonged, at the heart of Greece, in Athens.

Lilitu's words of the prophecy burned in his heart but he strove to push them aside dwelling only on his new position and territory. Things were going to change. And he was going to change them. He wasn't concerned about an old myth.

Vasile had told him everything about the pretender to his throne, the upstart protégée of Gregori who had created the means of his own destruction along with the destruction and cleansing of all but the Born of pure blood. He believed that he would take Gregori's place with the arrogance of his House, but it was his arrogance that would be his undoing. They would allow him the rope to create his own noose. And then the House of Tepes would rise supreme.

CHAPTER THIRTY: BRING THE GIRL

Vehicles outside the monastery walls would have announced the gathering to any who cared to venture there. But those that lived in proximity had long since barred their doors and windows.

Sister Maria had sent word to the outlying districts of the Feast Day but had silently prayed for them to stay away. Their lives and their souls depended on it.

In the dark cold of her cell, she prayed. She prayed that the sounds she had heard were born of fear and not reality. She had heard the opening and closing of a door opposite and the muffled sounds of someone receiving a beating and then the door opening and closing again. The retreating familiar footsteps told her that it was Santorini.

The scraping of iron in the lock meant that there was no entry for her to tend whoever was within. Her fingers worked the wooden rosary.

Santorini had changed his clothing, adopting a heavy black brocade frock coat and breeches in an effort to appear as one of them. He strode forwards to greet the latest guest. Drakos had arrived to be a part of the bargain. The anti HVV for the territory.

Drakos's penetrating black eyes briefly met Vasile's. Their understanding unspoken, Drakos extended his hand to Santorini.

"A pleasure to meet you and to hear of your achievement. Is there to be a demonstration? Or do we simply have your word on the properties of your creation?"

Santorini withdrew his hand. "Welcome, Drakos. Thank you for coming from Athens, I understand that you rarely leave the city. It is therefore an honour to receive you."

He led the way into the chapel that had undergone a serious transformation. The small wooden chairs occupied by the sisters during their devotions had been removed and replaced by elegant couches. In the centre of the chapel a large carved wooden table that served as their altar, was now spread with wine bottles, goblets and bowls of fruit. The latter for decoration and not sustenance. That would come later. The huge silver crucifix lay where it had been cast aside.

No-one had questioned Santorini's claim as Gregori's heir, allowing him the belief in order to bring out his ego, which in turn would lead him to revealing the secret of his serum. It was Drakos who first brought up the subject.

"So tell us, Santorini. Do you have a demonstration for us or not?"

"It would require the presence of one of the Created, and as we all know, this is a gathering of the Born."

The silence implied that they were all aware that one among them was most certainly not of the Born. Santorini was enraged but managed to keep cool. A created he may be, but he was created by Gregori and it was Gregori's blood that ran in his veins.

Markos Vasilakis diffused the situation. "That is certainly not an obstacle. As I understand it we have two guests who may qualify. I am certain it would be a pleasure for any one of us to turn one of them for you. Then we can see your handiwork."

Santorini was thoughtful. It was obvious his word alone would not be enough. They had to see for themselves. Well that was fine by him. He nodded assent at Markos.

Vasile Tepes picked up the thread. "Mircea, perhaps you would bring the girl to us."

Mircea smirked but left the room in silence. His anticipation in high gear, he hoped that he would be the one to have the pleasure. He ran his tongue over his elongated white canines. He could almost taste her.

Sister Maria heard his approach and stood against her door, straining to hear who it was and where he was going. The footsteps halted outside her room and for a heart stopping moment she thought it was her door that would be brutally thrust open. Instead she heard the lock being released opposite her. It was slightly further down the corridor from hers and she understood then. There were two prisoners.

She heard a small cry. A girl. Her heart froze as she immediately understood the implications and then shame engulfed her sending her to her knees clutching her rosary but unable to finger the prayers. How could she dare to intercede when it was she that had sheltered the evil, fearing for the life of her child? A child she had only seen fleetingly at her birth. But *her* child nevertheless. She had no doubt that Santorini wouldn't hesitate to suck the life blood from her daughter, no longer a child but a young woman. And she was right. Sister Maria was in torment.

She heard the girl being dragged from the room, and the whimper that came from the terrified voice. Her fingers were moving over the wooden beads without her realising it.

In nineteen years she had kept her promise and had never sought her daughter out, leaving her in the care of her adopted parents, devoting her life to God and the convent and unwittingly, Gregori. Now she was swamped with the desire to find her and warn her, to get her out of danger.

Sister Angelique had told her that the child's parents had given her the name Antheia, which meant 'flower' in Greek and she tried to visualise how she may now look. She wondered if the girl opposite looked like her daughter.

Her hands were on the door handle before she was aware of them.

The corridor was dark and silent but Maria was used to moving about soundlessly. The kitchen door stood ajar and she was inside in seconds. The window was larger than the ones in the cells and she could climb through with ease. The outer wall was a different matter. There was only one means of exit for her and that was through the front gate.

She slipped off her sandals and picked up the hem of her habit, unwilling to make any sound. Making her way silently around the outer wall she hoped that whatever was happening inside was keeping them focussed. Her heart was racing as she reached the front angle of the wall. Slowly, footstep by footstep she walked.

The night air was ripped by a series of tortured screams. Her imagination filled in the gap with a familiar sucking sound. Her hand was over her mouth to drown her own scream as she threw herself through the wooden gate.

The waning moon had appeared from under the thin clouds, giving light onto the dusty road. She ran until a pain in her chest made her bend forwards, gasping for breath. Gradually the pain subsided and her breathing began to return to normal and she stood upright.

The dark shadow seemed to materialise in front of her and a voice almost made her heart stop.

"Hello Sister Maria."

CHAPTER THIRTY ONE: A DAUGHTER

She tried to scream but no sound came from her and she felt her legs weaken then a rushing sound in her head just before she fainted.

Only moments later she opened her terrified eyes to look into the refined features of Mihai leaning over her. Other concerned faces gradually joined his and one in particular made her relax.

"Thank you, God," she whispered.

Beckett put his arm under her shoulders and helped her onto her feet.

Lane was looking at her in horror. "Maria … what happened to you?"

Maria's disfigured hand flew to her face. "The fire," she said, "I went back to rescue something. I … I'd rather not talk about it."

Beckett leaned forwards and drew her to him, planting a gentle kiss on her scars.

"Take your time Sister; tell us what's happening in there. Have you seen Darius? The young man who was with us last time?"

She shook her head. "I haven't seen him, but they have two people locked up. I … I'm afraid one of them has had a good beating. I heard it, but the door is locked and I couldn't get to whoever was in there."

Beckett went pale, "He's *got* to stop doing this, young idiot!" He exhaled long and hard. "I'm not waiting, I'm going in."

A restraining hand was on his arm before he could move. Mihai was staring hard at him.

"Wait, Beckett. We go in there without thinking, we're finished. They will already know we are coming because

179

they have Darius and they know we wouldn't leave him. While we wait, they will keep him alive."

"You don't know that, Mihai. While we wait, he's in there and they are doing God knows what to him." He wrenched his arm free of Mihai's grip and turned back to Sister Maria.

"What about a young girl?"

Maria dropped her head.

"Sister?"

She lifted her face slowly, and tears were falling down her scarred cheek. She let them fall.

"I'm sorry. I think that you are too late."

Muscles twitched along Lane's jaw line but she didn't speak.

"I think there are about twenty of them," Maria said, glancing around at them pointedly. "I overheard some of their conversation. I think they were waiting for someone to come from Athens."

Mihai looked at Lane, "Drakos."

"He must be here to take control of Gregori's territory," she replied.

Mihai nodded. "He was Gregori's son."

Beckett threw his hands in the air in exasperation. "Someone care to fill me in?"

Mihai nodded at him. "Drakos is Gregori's eldest son, and I mean eldest. He has inherited his father's territory by birthright but has to be seen to claim it by the other Houses. All rather formal. The House of Tepes and Vasilakis are present and probably the Popescu's and the Andros clan. All represented by their highest nobles, ha nobles! More like aristocratic thugs. All of them ruthless, all of them Born and all of them savage killers."

"And all of them are going to pay," Beckett said hoarsely.

Mihai's face was grim. "And some of them are dead already."

Maria cleared her throat, "The other one with the

mask, although he no longer wears it, is still there. He's been there ever since the night of the fire."

Beckett spun around, "You've given him shelter? Why? Why would you do that?"

"Because he was in need of care and because … because I have a daughter, Beckett. Adopted at birth but living just outside Parthavos, she is nineteen now and he knows where she is. He told me he would take a long time to drain her of all her blood..."

Lane put a hand on her shoulder. "Don't," she said, "It's okay, we know what he is."

Beckett was grinding his teeth.

"Is that where you were running to?" Lane asked.

Maria nodded.

"Then you'd better get going. How many other nuns are inside? "

Mihai shook his head. "No. The girl is safer if we deal with Santorini. And we are going to need all the help we can get. How many of the sisters are still in the monastery, Maria?"

"Only two now. He … killed Sister Teresa. Sister Agatha is still there, and Sister Anna. But Agatha is old and Anna is too young."

"Old or young they may be able to help," answered Mihai. "Let's go."

There was a low growl in Jude's throat.

"Hold that thought," Beckett said.

CHAPTER THIRTY TWO: THE TURNING

Angel lay like a waxwork on the tiled floor, her heart slowed to an imperceptible beat as it fluttered in her breast before it would finally concede defeat. Vasile Tepes had been waiting for the moment. He bit savagely into his own wrist and let the blood, almost black and viscous, fall into Angel's open mouth.

Drop by drop it splashed crimson against her teeth and lips before trickling down her throat. Now they would wait.

The wound on Vasile's wrist was already closing, but he checked his sleeve for stray blood. Satisfied that his appearance had not been compromised, he straightened his jacket sleeve and returned to the couch.

Drakos stood up. "So, Santorini, we shall soon see if what you promise is true."

"Of course it's true. Why would I have brought you all here if it weren't?" He looked down at Angel. "You won't have to wait much longer."

"And your price?"

"My price is Gregori's territory."

"I see. You presume to be Gregori's heir. But Gregori had a son. Did you not know that?"

Santorini stared at him. "No. I didn't. Who is he? Gregori never spoke of him but he did tell me that I would one day succeed him."

Drakos laughed. "Did he? Yes. Well, you should have learned that Gregori never, ever kept his promises. He never forgave his son for leaving the dreary life here for the life of the city. But to take his territory, the heir must first seek sanction from The Ancient One. Something else you appear not to know."

Santorini was well on the back foot, and he was beginning to feel threatened. "He told me that he was the oldest living of our kind."

Drakos was enjoying himself then. "Then he lied to you. Lilitu still lives, if living is what you would call it. She sleeps for centuries in a cave, looked after by a pathetic girl. But, nevertheless, the heir must seek her sanction."

"Then I'll go there."

Drakos laughed again and Markos and Vasile were grinning broadly.

"Sorry, I already did."

His words hit Santorini like the contents of a nail bomb.

Drakos stepped forwards. "Gregori was my father, and I have waited too long to take his territory. But not here. I will rule my territory from Athens; I couldn't bear not to see the Parthenon each day. I remember it being built. Yes, I *am* that old, and I *am* Gregori's heir. Now, I think we are all tired of waiting. Show us."

Santorini's hope then lay in his serum. He still had the formula and only one dose with him. They would still need him, and although his terms may have changed, he was still going to ask a high price.

A low moan came from Angel and she was writhing on the floor. The moan gave way to a scream of agony as the turning began.

Outside the perimeter wall at the rear of the building, Lane checked her weapons and leaped into the air, landing softly on top of the wall. Mihai followed and taking his cue from them, Jude stood back and ran at the wall, leaping high in the air and clearing it, landing in the courtyard ahead of the others, in mid transformation. Beckett shrugged, *what the hell*. He focussed his inner vision on the top of the wall, and leaped up. He landed beside Lane. "Well, what do you know?" he grinned.

They let themselves drop trying to create as little

disturbance as possible. Then they heard Angel's screams.

Sister Maria had told them the inner layout and their first priority was Darius. Lane knew the sounds of Angel's agony, they were too late, she had been fed and was turning and they would need Darius with them. She reached out and locked onto to him, he was alive. She breathed out softly, and nodded to Beckett. He understood. He raised his eyebrow at her and she knew his unspoken question. Angel. Lane shook her head.

Beckett was in the open kitchen window ahead of Lane, but of Mihai and Jude there was no sign having decided to go for the front. Mihai had told them that once inside they were to wait for his signal. Beckett slipped out into the corridor hoping to find Darius while Vasile and the others were focussed on Santorini at the other end, and he came face to face with Luca Tepes. His reflexes surprised even him as his long thin blade penetrated Luca's heart before he could utter a sound. He dragged him back into the kitchen and with several deft swipes of her scalpel; Lane cut out his heart and took off his head.

She crossed herself, and covered in his blood she followed Beckett back into the corridor. Sounds of Angel's agony echoed against the stone walls. Lane clamped her back teeth together. They would pay.

The key was still in the lock of Darius's door. Beckett felt an energy surge as he twisted it slowly. He felt the door give and leaned against it gently. It opened into darkness which Beckett's eyes quickly penetrated. Darius was lying in a heap on the floor, dried blood caked around his mouth and on his cheek. He appeared to be unconscious but as Beckett leaned over him, he stirred and opened his eyes.

"Beckett. Good to see you."

Beckett shook his head slowly, words of anger and reprimand flashing through his mind that would wait for later. Now was the time for relief, however temporary. Darius was beaten to shit but okay. *Déja vu*.

JAN McDONALD

"Darius, you need to know something. They have Angel."

As if to verify his words, another scream followed by a gut wrenching wail permeated the room. Darius leapt to his feet and fell back against Beckett as the room became a carousel. Bright lights were flashing behind his eyes, his eardrums were buzzing and his legs gave way.

"Easy there," said Beckett as he caught him and quickly clamped his hand over the boy's mouth as he sensed the anger building in the pit of his stomach.

Darius turned away from him. "It's my fault. I should have waited. I should have never let her follow me. Oh God."

"We all make mistakes. The important thing is putting them right."

"How? You tell me how I can put *that* right. I know those screams, they live in my nightmares. She's turning. Why the hell are we standing here?"

"Because we're waiting. Lane and Sabine are getting the other two nuns out of the way before the shit hits the fan. She had trouble with Sabine and when I last overlooked her she was laying Sabine out cold to protect her. No sense in jeopardising any …"

"Any more lives. You were about to say 'any more lives'."

He crumpled forwards and Beckett put his arm around him. "It's okay. We'll make it okay. Right now I need you to pull yourself together and stand with us again. Are you up to it?"

Darius nodded vigorously. "Fucking right I am."

"Eloquently put, Son."

The sound of a small explosion reached them, "Come on, that's Mihai. Showtime," he said as he tossed a hand gun to Darius, "I seem to remember you are a good shot."

186

CHAPTER THIRTY THREE: ALL HELL

Mihai had decided to split up and attack from front and rear. If nothing else it would half the force of their defence, and their timing had been right with the attention of those inside on Angel. He felt a sharp pang when he thought of her and hoped to hell Helena could help her. Images of the elfin faced young doctor brought an unaccustomed smile to his face and he suddenly felt more positive about the coming battle, for battle it would be.

Angel's screams had lodged in Jude's chest and he was angry. Facial hair was growing and his fingernails were protruding from bent hairy fingers. Mihai noted it.

"That's right, get angry, get *very* angry."

More pitiful screams came from the chapel and the low growl in Jude's throat grew louder and louder until his mouth was foaming, and then came the snarl. Bared savage teeth, beneath curled back lips, dripped saliva.

"Let's go" he snarled.

As they approached the open doorway two dark shadows emerged from the side of the house. Sentries. In one fluid movement Mihai leaped forwards and upwards followed swiftly by Jude. They were on the strolling guards in a millisecond. And in a movement so rapid that even the other vampires didn't track it, he had thrust his father's dagger straight into the heart of his victim. Jude was crouching in front of Mihai, his face a mass of hair and blood, and his victim lay to the side minus his throat. Vasile had chosen the wrong ones to guard the entrance.

Inside, Angel was in the throes of the turning and the flash skirmish outside hadn't reached their attention. Mihai put his hand in his pocket and pulled out a small ornate pistol. He leaped into the hallway and shot one of Vasile's entourage straight though the heart, the explosion causing the desired effect of temporary confusion.

Vasile was back in control in an instant; barking orders at the remainder of those of the House of Tepes. Drakos Vasilakis and Markos had taken instant control of the Greeks but Beckett and Darius were already upon the ones nearest the corridor. Lane swung her sword high and brought it crashing down onto one of their heads, pulled it free and swung again. The also rans were on the outside of the hoard, acting as shields for their Elders and another fell easily to Lane's sword.

Beckett was levelling his gun at Vasile when Mircea appeared from almost nowhere and took him to the ground. Darius leaped onto the wrestling pair and tried make contact with Mircea with the barrel of his gun. Mircea was screeching and hissing, teeth searching for their target as Darius's gun found its home and he squeezed the trigger hard.

Silver nitrate flooded Mircea and was instantly bringing him down. Vasile saw it and leaped high over the heads of the now seething mass of vampires. Darius couldn't track him and he appeared to suddenly materialise in front of him, sharp white canine teeth, black holes for eyes, and hands with the strength of ten men. Darius struck out with his knife trying to keep him at bay but quickly realised that Vasile was playing him. Drawing it out, savouring it. Angel screamed in agony again and in that instant Darius drew blood from Vasile's chest but missed his heart, and was going in for the second thrust when Vasile picked him up bodily and threw him hard against the wall before turning on Lane.

Markos Vasilakis, a stiletto in hand, focussed on Jude. He hesitated momentarily, assessing the options, on uncertain ground. Jude stood as upright as he could, sweat and blood glistening on his muscular chest as he too stopped and connected eye to eye. He turned his wolf hands palms upwards and made beckoning motions.

"Come on," was all he said.

Markos leaped at him and his long narrow blade plunged into Jude's shoulder. The rage inside was all it needed to complete his transformation into the snarling slavering savage beast that was his full potential. His hands had grown to almost twice their size, and his face seemed leaner, hungrier, covered in coarse animal hair that spread down onto his chest. His nostrils were flared and his eyes were burning caverns of amber light. He was past speech as the wolf inside had pushed Jude into the background and was in full attack. As Markos hurled himself at Jude, the wolf leaped to meet him and they collided mid air. The noise of the savagery of the wolf caused several of the younger vampires to stop. Two at least made for the exit. Jude realised what he had to do, he released control of the wolf and allowed it free reign, from then on he would have no power over it, conceding dominance to the now Alpha part of him. He knew that from then on wolf would be the dominant one. He had sacrificed what was left of his control on the beast within and would have to live with the consequences. Whatever they were.

Markos was no match for the ravening wolf and soon lay in a heap. Jude jumped over him and flew forwards towards Drakos who had been getting the better of Beckett. Hearts were racing and adrenaline pumping through veins, enhancing, strengthening, crazing. Jude's jaws clamped over Drakos's arm, and teeth sank into almost bloodless flesh. He spat the severed muscle onto the ground and was on him again, a biting, ripping, growling mass of hair, teeth and claws. A pistol shot rang out and he felt the bullet bite into his shoulder below the stab wound. In a frenzied howl of pain and rage, the wolf was out of control.

Blood slicked the floor and spatters were appearing on the white painted walls. The scent of the blood crazing the vampires fuelled by rage was heavy and cloying in the air.

Mihai had dispatched two of the lesser Vasilakis clan

and was striking at a third when he caught sight of Angel, on her knees now and crawling slowly towards them, red lights in her eyes and she was hissing. In that instant of hesitation he was overpowered and heading for the floor. The other vampire was on him in a heartbeat, fangs bared and aiming at his throat. The glint of steel behind his assailant scarcely had time to register before Darius's blade bit home and severed the head and neck. Covered in blood he turned in time to see Angel fixing him in a red glare.

"Dariusss," she hissed. "Dariusss. Help me, Dariusss."

He dropped his knife in horror and staggered backwards towards the front door. He was undone.

Inch by inch she crawled towards him, hissing, and pleading in a high pitched whine, then something snapped inside and he yanked Beckett's gun from his pocket. "I'm so sorry, Angel. So very sorry."

He aimed the barrel directly between her eyes and began to squeeze.

"No! Darius don't!" Helena was there then, her voice loud and commanding as she ran forwards and hit Angel between the shoulder blades with a loaded syringe. Jo was at her side then and they were pulling Angel free of the chaos and out into the night.

Darius was stunned and was about to follow when he caught a glimpse of Santorini in a darkened corner, watching the battle and waiting. Waiting for the obstacle to him becoming Gregori's heir to die.

"You filthy fucking coward!" he yelled as he dived after him.

Santorini turned on him in an instant, blood suffusing his eyes, rage and hatred oozing from every pore. "You!" He spat onto the floor and launched himself forwards at Darius, canines down ready, and long sharp lancets on every finger. He slashed at Darius's face, leaving long red trails on his cheek, then came back at him aiming for his throat.

"I don't think so, you bastard," yelled Beckett as he

threw himself between the two. The razor sharp lancets were a hair's breadth away from his heart as Beckett pumped four successive rounds into him, filled with the silver nitrate and small explosive charge. As Santorini fell onto his knees, his face was filled with disbelief. In slow motion he fell forwards and lay in a spreading pool of crimson.

"Is he dead? Really dead this time?" panted Darius.

Beckett stood over him and put his hand over Darius's and together they plunged the boy's blade straight through the middle of his heart with such a force that it shattered the tiles beneath.

"He is now."

The room was like a scene from Dante's inferno with bodies scattered around them. With Markos dead the House of Vasilakis had decided on the better part of valour and buggered off into the night leaving Drakos and Jude in a rolling turmoil of blood and teeth. Darius took his knife and pounced onto Drakos's back, bringing the blade over his head and wrenching it backwards.

Gregori's heir was dead.

Beckett was leaping towards Vasile who was poised above Lane with her own sword pointing down towards her chest.

"Nooo!" he screamed as he landed in front of Vasile in time to see the sword go through bone and sinew and flesh.

Everything appeared to stop as if the world had ceased to turn and time was stilled. The scene was surreal and blurred and sounds became muffled and far away. He lunged at Vasile who was already half way out of the door. All eyes were on Lane and everything was in slow motion, Darius had fallen to his knees and Mihai stood with a stunned expression, motionless except for the blood dripping from his dagger. Jude was crouched on all fours, panting and growling low, burning amber eyes slowly darkening, returning to their indigo hue.

The howl of rage and torment that rent the air came from Beckett as he lifted Lane into his arms where she lay like a bloodied rag doll.

CHAPTER THIRTY FOUR: THE GOD OF HIS ABANDONMENT

A deep pain had lodged in Beckett's heart and his tears fell unchecked as he stumbled from the chapel with his precious burden. No one else moved, too shocked to comprehend their loss. He had no idea of where he was going; only that he had to take her from that place.

From out of nowhere Sister Maria was before him. She laid her hand gently on Lane's brow. "Bring her to my room," she said.

Beckett followed her, grateful for direction. He laid Lane on the small bed and she opened her eyes.

"So, Handsome, how did we do?"

He nodded through his tears. "We did okay. They have all gone. Darius and I settled with Santorini, and Jude, well Jude put the shit up me, let alone them. A few of them legged it and the last I saw of Vasile he was heading for cover. Don't speak now, you need to rest and recover."

He stroked her hair, matted with blood, some of it hers, some not. Her wounds were deep and lethal and continued to ooze the red stuff. He stared in desperation trying to stem the bleeding from one wound to the other. Her breathing was laboured and her eyes were once again closed although her hand was tightly clasped around Beckett's.

He didn't hear Mihai enter the room behind him. Or the quiet sobbing from Darius.

He was in the zone, focussed, in a comfortable place that he had shunned for years. In a place where there was peace and understanding. He was on his knees at the side of her, her hand clasped between his and he was praying. Praying as he never had before. Not pleading, not demanding; just seeking an understanding with the one who had made the plan. He offered and made no bargain, his prayers were for her soul and he could feel the brilliance of it, see it, even through closed eyes.

She coughed and red bubbles appeared at the corner of her mouth and he wiped them away with his fingertips.

"She needs to sleep," said Mihai. "It's her only chance, deep vampire sleep while her body heals."

As if to concur, Lane opened her eyes again and smiled at Beckett. "I love you, Handsome."

Beckett cleared his throat, "I think I've always loved you, Legs. But it wasn't right, then."

"And now?"

"Now you won't have to watch me grow old. You won't have to grieve for me because of old age. Now we are equals."

She tried to nod but it made her cough red bubbles again. "I know. I couldn't have born that pain. I need to sleep Beckett. And I don't know for how long. I think it will be long."

He stroked her head and kissed her blood stained lips as reverently as if he were drinking from a holy chalice. "As long as it takes. I'll be here. Waiting for you."

She smiled and her facial muscles relaxed as she slipped into the depths of vampire sleep.

He spoke to her, lovingly and softly but her ears couldn't hear, she was out of his reach and he would have to wait. He didn't care for how long.

Mihai put his hand on his shoulder and gripped tightly. Beckett didn't move. He heard Darius still weeping and turned to him. "Don't," he said. "She isn't gone. Just sleeping. We'll take her home."

Mihai gripped his shoulder even more tightly. "No, Beckett. She's too weak. It would be the end to take her from here."

"But ..."

"I will take care of her," the small young voice,

wracked with emotion, interrupted him. He looked up to see the young Sister Anna, her tear stained face betraying the loss of her innocence. She had seen too much for one so young.

"I promise you, Beckett. I will spend my days caring for her, until she is ready to wake. There will be no violence, no blood shed, and no blood lust. When she needs sustenance, I will feed her. Please allow me to do this."

His eyes penetrated hers and he read her and he knew that this was the right thing to do. He nodded. "I will make sure you have all you need."

"As will I," said Mihai.

It was too much for Darius and he had left the room, still in shock and in search of Angel. He didn't know how much more he could take.

Mihai nodded to Beckett and left.

In the minutes that followed Beckett understood. If he had expected an angel's trumpet or divine bright light, he would have been sadly disappointed. As it was, the warmth began somewhere in the middle of his chest and slowly spread throughout his body. His soul was alight with prayer and he reached out to the God of his abandonment, communing on behalf of her soul and her healing.

And the God of his abandonment answered him.

Anna was behind him then, a small bowl of water in her hand.

"Please allow me."

He nodded his acceptance and knew that in that acceptance came his own redemption and his salvation.

He stood to allow her close and Anna smiled at him. Gently she washed the congealing blood from Lane's face and softly smoothed the dark chestnut hair from her face. She was whispering to her as a mother to a child although he could not hear the words and refrained from the intrusion of locking onto her voice. Lane was in good hands.

He bent forwards and laid his lips on hers. "Sleep well, my love." As he stood upright again, his eyes fell onto the pocket watch that Lane always wore on a chain around her neck. He gently lifted it over her head and put it in his pocket. I'll watch the time for both of us."

Beckett turned to leave. Anna's expression was questioning.

"There are things to do," he said. "It isn't over until … well, it isn't over yet."

CHAPTER THIRTY FIVE: THE STORM BRINGER

The gathering in the chapel was a sombre group. Sabine had been released from the enforced unconsciousness imposed by Lane when she had slipped away from him, and now she was on her knees mopping pools of fast congealing blood from the chapel floor alongside Maria. Jude sat in the corner, gradually relinquishing the hold of the wolf, exhausted and shocked.

Mihai strode to meet Beckett, looking grim.

"I can't tell you how sorry, I am, Beckett. But while she sleeps, there's hope."

Beckett's cheek muscles twitched as he fought the tears. "I know, " he said quietly.

"Stay here, my friend. I will take care of what has to be done now."

Beckett understood. Dead they may be, but unless the vampires were dealt with in the old way, they would rise on the following day. The gristly task was not beyond him but Mihai was insistent.

"I will see to it."

A soft lilting voice behind him made him spin around.

"I'll help you." Helena stood close to Mihai, her eyes reaching into his, comprehension and compassion evolved to a new level. "Please."

Mihai smiled in gratitude and something else. Something that suddenly seemed too precious to be let go. "Thank you. I would appreciate that."

She smiled a half smile and stepped back outside.

Beckett was suffused with an inner peace that he had not known for years. "I will do what is necessary when you've finished."

Mihai beamed at him. "I knew you would. Thank you Beckett."

"The Church is no longer a part of me, but I believe you. Once a priest always a priest."

Mihai nodded. "You will be *our* priest, Father. And welcome. There is no need of a Church, and religion is dying. Connection to a higher power of whatever name is a personal thing. Will you wear the collar?"

"I don't know, perhaps until she wakes."

Mihai was ahead of him. "There are no conditions here Beckett, and celibacy and loneliness would certainly not be one of them. She will be proud of you."

Sister Maria was behind him then, her hand outstretched with her own wooden rosary.

"Take this, Father. Say your own prayers with it, whatever they may be; they will reach the same place."

He smiled his thanks and hugged her. "Thank you Maria, but I would rather you kept it and prayed for us all." Where he had just come from no icons or symbolic jewellery were necessary, no pomp, pageantry and long frocks. It had been one to one.

"Where's Angel?" His question met with silence. "No. Oh no. Where is she?"

Mihai was grim, "She's outside with Helena and Jo. I don't know if she's going to make it, Beckett."

Beckett strode outside as lilac fingers were reaching across the dawn sky. Jo was sitting cross legged with Angel draped across him, cradled in his arms like a small child. His eyes were closed and he was chanting in Navajo. Helena had her fingers around Angel's wrist looking grave.

She looked up as Beckett and Mihai approached.

"I took a chance," she said. "It was all I could think of. She went down like a stone; I hope to God I haven't killed her."

Mihai put his hand on her shoulder. "She was already dead," he said. "Turned by one of the Undead, she would have risen tomorrow night. And what would have been

198

done to her then would be worse. You did the right thing, and thank God, you did. It may save her, it may not. But you gave it a shot. We must just watch and wait now. How is she doing?"

Helena shrugged. "Her pulse is deathly slow but it's strong, her breathing is barely discernable."

"Can you leave her? I could use your offer of help."

Helena got to her feet and watched Jo and Angel for several moments and then moved close to Mihai.

"I believe I know what is expected of me. I'm a long way from being a surgeon, but I'll do my best. With you to help me through it."

Mihai smiled at her, a smile that reached his eyes and her heart. He put his arm around her and they walked slowly together into the gloomy chapel, Beckett followed several paces behind them.

One by one they carried the bodies of the dead vampires from the chapel into the tiny garden at the rear. Mihai struck the first blow, deftly removing the head of Mircea as Beckett intoned the ancient prayers that would seek to release the soul. Helena swallowed hard and closed her eyes. She opened them to see Mihai removing Mircea's heart. In the distance thunder rolled. *Fabulous* she thought. *Sound effects.*

She watched as one of Vasile's cousins was despatched the same way. "Okay," she said, "I'm ready."

Her hands were trembling imperceptibly as she bent over the body of one of the Vasilakis dead, blade in shaking hand. Thunder rolled again, nearer this time. "There's a storm coming," she whispered to no-one in particular.

Mihai's face was devoid of expression as he concentrated with grim determination on the gristly job in hand. One by one the vampires were laid to rest. As Drakos's body lay at Mihai's feet, massive raindrops began to fall and bounce off the hardened ground, soaking them in seconds. The dawn sky had darkened to midnight and the distant thunder became not so distant. Mihai looked up at the sky as a terrible realisation began to slowly dawn.

"Get inside! Quickly. And tell the others to get inside and lock and bolt the doors and windows!"

Helena was about to protest that she wasn't afraid of a storm and anyway she was already soaked to the skin, but one look at Mihai made her turn and run inside, calling the others as she ran.

Beckett stood firm, "Mihai?"

Mihai looked up at the blackened sky again, "Listen." He raised Lane's sword and cut clean through Drakos's neck, severing the head from the body. Thunder rumbled loudly close by.

Beckett frowned.

Mihai bent over the torso of Drakos and began to cut out his heart.

Lightening crackled and forked to earth.

"Shit!" Mihai exploded. "Help me finish here, Beckett. We must burn the bodies while we can and give them a decent end to indecent lives."

"The rain will put out any fire, Mihai. Can't it wait until the storm is passed?"

"The storm isn't going to pass. It's coming here. Help me light the fire."

Beckett had emptied the monastery generator of its petrol and in silence he poured the entire contents over the bodies. Mihai flicked a cigarette lighter into flame and tossed it onto the gruesome remains. With a whoosh the flames licked and flickered, growing in size and ferocity until Mihai and Beckett were driven backwards by the intense heat. Not a garden any more, but a crematorium.

Beckett stared wordlessly at Mihai, searching his face for explanation.

"Lilitu. Someone has woken The Ancient One."

"I thought The Ancient One was myth."

Mihai shook his head. "Lilitu is part demon, part vampire; she's the oldest vampire alive. Though alive isn't the best way to describe her, she sleeps for many centuries at a time. Only a handful of our kind knows where to find her and that doesn't include me. She's a fierce protector of the evil ones. She's Sumerian and is still there, although it's Iraq now. She's known as the Storm Bringer. You probably know her better as Lilith."

Thunder and lightening filled the electric air. Fork lightening ripped through the inky sky, reaching its electrically charged fingers to the ground, illuminating the entire valley with an electric blue and pink light show accompanied by breaking thunder akin to an explosion.

The petrol was doing its job as an accelerant and the funeral piers were defeating the rain.

Mihai grabbed Beckett and dragged him inside. He banged the door behind them and slammed the bolt home. They dragged a wooden cabinet against the door as Mihai shook his head.

"I don't know why I'm doing this; doors are no barrier to her. Come on, we need to warn the others."

Helena had ushered the others inside. Darius was still ashen and hadn't left Angel's side. There was no obvious change in her and she was as pale as death. Helena stood to meet them, "Her pulse is stronger and is slightly quicker," she said. Her eyes met Mihai's, "Tell me," she said.

Jude and Sabine were sitting wrapped in each others arms, kissing and oblivious to everything except themselves, Sabine put her head on his shoulders and Beckett could see that his body had resumed its human form. Thunder crashed overhead and the rain had mutated into huge hailstones, slamming into the walls and windows. The lightening followed one crack after another, relentless and without mercy.

Sabine was shaking and pale despite Jude's efforts to comfort her. Sister Maria was fingering the wooden beads as her lips moved silently through the prayers that were a part of her, as surely as if they had been her breath.

Angel lay on the floor with Jo kneeling by her side, holding her hand, and Helena was next to Darius, her arm around his shoulders.

Lightening forked again accompanied by the incessant bangs of raging thunder. There was a loud crash and the sound of falling masonry. The bell tower had gone and so had part of the roof.

In a shroud of lightening that lit up the chapel a figure landed in front of them and slowly, very slowly, with a roar of rage, stood upright.

Lilitu was among them.

CHAPTER THIRTY SIX: LAST STAND

In a flurry of dust, rubble and flame she stood before them.

As they stood in shock Lilitu's parchment skin and skeletal appearance began to change. She grew taller and her sagging breasts and skin filled out. Her wings were outstretched flapping her rage, and her feminine face gave way to the demon inside. She roared her fury at the killing of some of the highest nobles of the pure blood.

She pointed a bony claw at Mihai, hissing at him, her eyes ablaze.

"You! You are one of the Born, how dare you commit such an offence? You will pay." Her voice echoed above the cacophony of the storm which continued to batter the tiny monastery.

She flew at him emitting a high pitched, strident cry like that of a demented screech owl. Even to the vampires she moved beyond sight and had laid open Mihai's chest before they even saw it.

Beckett, Darius and Jude all reacted simultaneously.

Beckett had grabbed Lane's sword and was lunging impotently as Lilitu moved so quickly she avoided every thrust. Darius pointed Beckett's pistol at her but failed to track her movements. He daren't fire in case he hit one of the others but kept the butt pointed at her, waiting for the clear shot. He waited too long and found himself held in the bony claw, picked up like a rag doll and heading for the yellowed fangs.

Beckett took the opportunity to hit his target and the sword was buried deep in Lilitu's abdomen. A foul stench filled the air making them gag and retch. He hit again and again, but as each hit caused damage, the other wounds

203

were already healing. And Darius was still held in the vice like grip of the clawed hand, tossed about in her rabid rage.

Helena dragged Mihai away from the violence and bent over him, shaking from head to foot. Her trembling hands found the massive wound and although it was huge, it didn't appear too deep. His vital organs looked in tact but he was losing too much blood. She pulled off her shirt and pressed it hard to the wound. "Mihai, you listen to me. I just found you and I'm not going to let you off the hook this easily." Her shirt was already crimson soaked and her hands were fast becoming covered in his blood. "Mihai!"

As Beckett prepared to strike again, Sister Maria was in front of him and she threw her wooden rosary into the demon's face. There was a fresh roar of fury and her bony hand was swiping through the air. Darius was dropped in a heap and Sister Maria had replaced him in the foul talons. With a sickening crunch, Maria's neck was broken and she was cast aside as Lilitu took to the air, wildly flapping the leathery wings, eyes ablaze and homing in on Beckett who was slashing frantically at her. It was like trying to cut through mist, she moved so fast.

He leaped into the air, trying for a higher target, but she evaded him deftly. Landing on his feet, he instantly leaped again, swinging the sword as he did so. It failed to make contact.

From the far corner of the room, a deep growl was growing into a savage roar, as Jude once more called on the wolf inside him. His transformation was almost instant and suddenly he was flying at Lilitu, savage jaws and claws ripping and tearing as he landed on her back, vicious teeth ripping into yellowed flesh.

Beckett took his cue and struck her again, full on in the belly. For a split second, Lilitu was still and then with a flash of twisting movements she was trying to dislodge Jude from her neck. But his teeth held fast and Lilitu's blood, black as ink, was spattering the floor. But still she raged as lightening streaked through the hole in the roof blasting the floor as it hit.

Mihai's open chest wound had stopped leaking blood and appeared to be closing, albeit slowly. Helena, continued to press hard on the wound as a low moan came from his lips. He couldn't speak but she knew instinctively what he wanted from her. Pressing her shirt hard onto the wound was actually preventing his wound from closing. She pulled it away, her heart doing somersaults, and she held her breath as Mihai's wound began to heal.

Lilitu continued to try and dislodge Jude and eventually he was sent to the floor. With a screech of triumph, Lilitu moved in.

Jude was exhausted and shaking but the wolf was unbowed. He was on his feet in an instant and leaping at Lilitu's throat.

Thunder and lightening continued to crash around them illuminating the scene of carnage. Jude fought with all he had left as the demon screeched and hissed and slashed at him.

Lilitu suddenly froze, the screech on her lips unuttered. Everyone was still, watching and wondering as slowly, very slowly, Lilitu staggered and fell forwards.

At that moment, the final fork of lightening lit up the beleaguered chapel. Beckett stood behind her, chest heaving and his breath coming in laboured gasps, and sticking from her back, at a crazy angle, was the huge silver crucifix from the chapel's altar. Beckett had used such force it had crushed the ancient ribs and penetrated her heart and lungs, and the silver was already reacting with her vampire cells.

He fell on to his knees, unable to speak, simply staring at the fallen Lilitu. Demon she may have been, but dead demon she now was.

The storm abated as quickly as it had grown and the clear light of the dawn was reaching into the chapel through the window.

"Helena," Jo said in a low voice. "Come. Look."

Angel's face was a pale pink instead of the deathly grey of recent hours and her breathing was steady. Helena felt her pulse and smiled. "She's going to be all right. You know what that means? We're on the right track. I'm certain that giving the dose at the very moment she turned had everything to do with it, but we're on the right track, I know it. If I work more on the gene silencing, I think that will crack it."

Darius struggled to his feet, winded and battered from his previous beating but otherwise unscathed. He limped over to the far corner of the room and picked up the wooden rosary that lay where Lilitu had hurled it in fury. He spent several moments just holding it and then he hung it around his neck. "Thank you, Sister," he said. He lifted his head and walked painfully over to Angel and knelt beside her.

"Hey, Angel. Wake up. You owe me a drink."

Beckett was on his feet, staggering forwards with Lane's sword raised high. In one savage blow Lilitu's head parted company with the rest of her body. He threw the sword onto the floor and walked out of the chapel.

CHAPTER THIRTY SEVEN: BLESSING WAY

The door to Lane's room stood ajar and he gently pushed it wide.

She lay like a statue. At her bedside he stood holding her hand; calmer than he could ever remember.

"Well, you missed out on some heavy shit, Legs. I mean a bloody demon for God's sake. Lilitu. Mihai said she was The Ancient One. *Was*, being the operative word, thanks to Jude. You should have seen him, or the wolf, or both of them, hell, I don't know one from the other any more. Remind me never to piss him off. He was the one who saved our collective arses, gave me time to finish her off. I'm so sorry my love, but we couldn't save Maria. Jude and Jo are burying her now and then I'll go and see to her. She saved Darius's life, but it cost her own. We paid a high price tonight.

"Angel looks like she'll make it, and the boy is okay. She'll sort him out once she's on her feet again. Mihai took a bad hit but he's healing, and our Dr Helena looks like she'll make it her business to see that he does. I didn't see that coming did you? But I think they're well suited. Her serum looks as though it's going to work, though she says it needs tweaking, whatever that means." He paused, unable to contain his emotions in mere commentary.

"I don't want to leave you here. You know that. But Mihai said we couldn't move you and I believe him. I'm not going to take the chance."

His voice cracked and he took a deep breath.

"I have to go back with them, love. But I'll be back as soon as I can. Please believe me, I wouldn't leave you here unless I had to, there are still things that need to be finished. You take your time and sleep and heal, because when you wake up, I'm going to be here. "

His tears were hot on his cheek as he bent to kiss her but he was saved from sobbing openly as Darius stood in the doorway gently tapping on the door.

"Is it okay for me to come in? The others are getting ready to leave and I just wanted … well, I just wanted to …"

His words failed him as Beckett put his arm around him. "She knows, son."

Sister Anna stood outside head down, hands crossed in front of her.

"Sister, we will see to the repairs and there will always be enough funds sent to you to keep this place and to look after her. Get help from the village if you need it. We will also make arrangements for that … that obscenity of a silver shrine to be taken from here. I know you're a closed order but I need to be able to speak with you regularly."

Anna raised her hand to stop him. "There *is* no order now, just her and me. I promised you I would look after her and I'll stay here for as long as she needs me. You can leave me your cell phone and only you will know how to contact me. I will speak with you as often as you need. You should go now and let me take care of her."

"Why would you do this?"

"We all have our purpose, and perhaps this is mine." She dropped her head, effectively ending the conversation.

Mihai was on his feet and leaning on Helena when they returned to the chapel.

"You can do the honours so we can get rid of it," he said to Beckett.

Beckett nodded and moved over to what remained of Lilitu, whose body had already begun to collapse into slimy decay. He threw both arms around the silver crucifix and heaved it from her body, ignoring the sucking noise it made. It was light in his arms as he took it outside to a stone trough that was now full, courtesy of the rainstorm.

Immersing it in the crystal clear water, he blessed it as he removed the contamination.

Inside, Darius had been one step ahead of him and had replaced the upturned altar awaiting the cross. Beckett strode purposefully to it and placed it centrally. Sabine had found some candles and placed them on either side. Beckett lit them.

When he turned around, they were all standing with their heads bowed. He swallowed the hard lump in his throat.

Jude and Sabine had dragged the foul remains outside and already the flames were doing their work. They stood arms tight around each other. There would be no prayers over Lilitu; her soul had long since been claimed by the abyss.

Beckett drew a deep breath in, "Well, I guess we're ready.

It took only an hour to clear out of the hotel in Parthavos and the network had lived up to expectations at Kozani airport. The journey home was solemn as they were locked in their individual thoughts and grief. They had lost a lot that night and Vasile Tepes was still out there.

Mihai had decided to go with them; he had business with a certain red headed geneticist with elfin features.

The Cedars felt cold and empty, it already missed her, but her presence was everywhere, comforting and reassuring. Beckett stood in her consulting room and decided to move his old chair behind her desk; he would keep vigil from there. He opened the ornate cigarette case on the leather top and took one, lighting it with her matching lighter.

"Well, it's hardly going to kill me is it?" he asked aloud.

Darius was behind him before he realised it, his mind was many miles across the Aegean.

"Hey," Darius said, "It's time."

They were all assembled in the Hogan waiting for him.

209

Jo was about to perform the Blessing Way ceremony on Jude. He wore his old bandana and there was a still, calm atmosphere inside the Hogan. He had placed the oak boughs in the four corners to announce to the Holy People that a ceremony was about to take place. Pungent herbs were smoking on the central fire. And several small bowls were on the floor, each containing different coloured ground vegetable material, pollen, flowers, and cornmeal. Next to them lay a large white buckskin ready for the sand painting that would be an important part of the ceremony.

"Blessing Way takes several days and nights," Jo said, "And as the Enemy Way rite was ended before its time it is important that we honour this. " he turned to Sabine, "You should wear the shawl, child. It is symbolic. In the tradition of my people, the Dine,☐ it is worn by the wife of the one who seeks healing from The Holy Ones. Great healing will take place here, allowing this man and wolf to walk together in harmony. Neither one nor the other in dominance. It is well with this man that you wear the symbol of his wife."

Sabine flushed and drew the shawl tightly around her as if it had indeed been Jude's arms.

Jo began the first chant as Jude lay on the floor covered once more with pine branches and flower heads. Singing to Mother Earth, or Changing Woman, Jo sang as he began to sprinkle the fine colours from the bowls onto the buckskin.

His chants brought calm to them as they listened and watched as Jo created images that took away their breath.

The four principal colours of white, blue, yellow and black, were symbolic of the directions: white with the dawn and the east, blue with the midday sky and the south, yellow with evening twilight and the west, and black with the night sky and the north. He laid the colours using his right hand and allowed the material to trickle out between his thumb and forefinger. Dimensions and balance between certain figures had to be exact in order for the sand painting to be effective, for the proper balance to be achieved. He kept the figures that were emerging in proper alignment with pieces of string as he created images of The Holy People to insure their presence and aid in the ceremony.

The sandpainting was oriented so that the top was in the east and surrounded by a guardian on the other three sides, protecting it from evil, allowing strength and all good things which come from the east with the dawn to enter. For three days and nights he chanted to Earth Mother and Sky Father, seeking healing from The Holy Ones for the man who was now his friend. Jude slept for most of the time waking only for sips of water and to eat a mouthful of bread.

When the sandpainting was finished it portrayed the figures of The Holy Ones, along with traditional symbolism, representations of the sacred mountains and at the foot of Earth Mother and Sky Father a wolf joined with a man encircled in scared Navajo icons. The painting itself moved them all.

At the end of the third day, Jo knew it was time for the night chant and after they were all refreshed, he began the last of his songs. His voice and the rattle and drum put them all in place far removed from the carnage and grief that they had left behind.

Jude awoke just before dawn and Beckett could see the change that had taken place while he journeyed with The Ancient Ones and The Holy People. He remembered Sister Anna's words, '*We all have a purpose …perhaps this is mine*'. Jude knew his purpose and as Beckett looked around him at Mihai and Helena, Jude and Sabine, Darius and Angel, his heart opened wide as he reached across the ocean to a small monastery in Greece. He had a purpose now and would fulfill it while he waited for her and he thanked God for it.

As dawn gave way to morning sun, he sat next to Jude.

"Do you still mean to return to Tora Bora?"

Jude nodded. "But first I mean to have me a Gypsy wedding. We were sort of hoping you would do the honours, Beckett. "

Beckett flushed with pleasure, "I'd love to, but I'm no longer an ordained priest, it wouldn't be legal."

Jude shrugged, "Piece of paper. It has no meaning to me, or her. It is what is in the heart that matters. So, will you?"

Beckett grinned at him. "It will be my pleasure. Then I will come with you to Tora Bora. I've a lot of time to kill."

"And then?" asked Jude.

"And then I have an appointment with Vasile Tepes."

THE END

Beckett's adventures continue in the third part of the trilogy due in 2015.

If you would like to be notified when the next book is released, be sure to follow the link below to sign up to my mailing list:

http://janmcdonaldemailsign-up.gr8.com/

THANK YOU!

To my Reader:

Many thanks for buying *Lycan*, I hope you enjoyed reading it.

If you did enjoy it, please post a review at Amazon, Goodreads or your favourite social network site and let your friends know about *Lycan*.

I hope that this has whetted your appetite to read my other novels. You can find details of these in the next few page as well as my short story collections.

Happy Reading!
All the best
Jan

ALSO BY JAN MCDONALD

The Beckett Vampire Trilogy
Midnight Wine: getBook.at/midnightwine

Part 3 coming 2015

Mike Travis Paranormal Investigations
The Crowsmoor Curse: getBook.at/Crowsmoorcurse

Long Shadows: getBook.at/longshadows

The Sacred Ark: getBook.at/sacredark

The Haunted Diary of Victoria Little:
getBook.at/haunteddiary

The Merlin Manuscript: getBook.at/merlin

The Sin Eater: getbook.at/sineater

Mike Travis short stories

Beginnings: getBook.at/Beginnings

Halloween: getBook.at/halloween

Christmas Spirits: getBook.at/christmasspirits

ABOUT JAN MCDONALD

Jan lives close to the Welsh borders which have their own mystical quality and provide endless resources in the way of legends and folklore surrounding paranormal experiences. She loves all things paranormal and has read the best: Dennis Wheatley, Stephen King, Edgar Allan Poe, Bram Stoker and all those authors that excel in the creepy or downright scary world of paranormal events.

When she embarked on the Mike Travis series, she realised that the field of paranormal investigation is more than we see on the popular TV programmes. So in order to provide compelling ghost hunting tales but with the greatest accuracy, Jan trained as a Paranormal Investigator and has studied parapsychology.

CONTACT DETAILS

Visit the authors website: jan-mcdonald.co.uk

Follow on Twitter: @janmcdonald1

Like on Facebook: Jan-McDonald-Author

Cover designed by: Raven Crest Books

Published by: Raven Crest Books
www.ravencrestbooks.com

Follow us on Twitter:
www.twitter.com/lyons_dave

www.ingramcontent.com/pod-product-compliance
Lightning Source LLC
Chambersburg PA
CBHW071334250626
47159CB00004B/1592